Choke Points

The characters, with two exceptions, and events in this book are fictitious. Any similarity to real persons (with the exception of Lee Hunt and Todd Busch), living or dead is coincidental and not intended by the author.

All rights reserved. No part of this book may be reproduced in any form or by any electronic or mechanical means without written permission from the author, except by a reviewer who may quote brief passages in a review.

Cover design by Sunny Su (sunnysu@graphicartists.com)

Web site design by Lisa Adams (www.lisaadams.com)

Printed in the United States of America by Cutter Publishing (www.cutterpublishing.com)

Copyright © 2008 Mike Walling
All rights reserved.
ISBN: 0-615-25865-4
ISBN-13: 978-0615258652

Visit www.cutterpublishing.com to order additional copies.

Choke Points

A NOVEL BY

Mike Walling

2008

To Barbara,
Thanks for your
support and friendship
Mike Walling

Choke Points

ACKNOWLEDGEMENTS

This book could not have been written without the generous assistance of several experts.

Paul Burns reviewed the scenarios and provided a rare inside view of international shipping and freight forwarding.

Kevin Smith, a former US Marine, also reviewed the scenarios and provided details of Iraqi Intelligence under Saddam Hussein.

Lee Hunt's expertise in mine and counter-mine warfare was invaluable in writing that scenario. Fortunately he is well aware of the destruction mines can inflict and, along with the Navy's NMAWC, is working diligently to prevent such an attack.

The field of large vessel marine salvage is highly specialized and often dangerous. Todd Busch, Vice President & General Manager, TITAN Salvage, LLC (www.titansalvage.com), provided a wealth of information on current techniques.

Tyl Hewitt, a long time friend, provided the description of Rock Creek Park used in the ambush scene.

Lieutenant Lesley Lykins, USN, Deputy, Navy Office of information, East, assured me that the information used from the Official U.S. Navy SEAL Information Web Site (www.sealchallenge.navy.mil/seal/introduction.aspx) is Public Domain.

Sincere thanks to Robin Smith (www.robinsmithink.com) who went above and beyond the call of duty in editing the manuscript. As always, her cogent comments and sharp eye were invaluable in shaping this book.

My loving and lovely wife, Mary, provided unwavering support through yet another long project.

To all the men and women dedicating their lives to ensure this never occurs.

WASHINGTON, Aug 01, 2002 (United Press International via COMTEX)

Despite the challenges faced in securing America's ports and maritime trade infrastructure since Sept. 11, the Coast Guard is up to the task, Thomas H. Collins, the new Commandant of the United States Coast Guard, said in a speech on July 30.

Collins said the agency also plays an important economic role by protecting international trade. He said that more than 95 percent of foreign trade passes through the nation's seaports, and that maritime trade overall contributes $1 trillion to the gross domestic product.

Collins believes that with thousands of ships and millions of containers entering U.S. ports annually, maritime transportation is a likely terrorist target.

He added that the potential economic impact of a major shutdown in water traffic would make the "9/11 aviation shutdown pale in comparison."

00

Sunday

Norfolk, Virginia, 1:00 PM Eastern Time

A low haze hung over the water as the 567-foot Navy cruiser USS *Concord* eased her way up Thimble Shoals Channel.

"It's been a long nine months, but we're almost there," *Concord*'s captain, Bill Wallace said to his Officer of the Deck, Lieutenant Debra Hearn. "How are your daughters doing?

"They're doing okay, but it's been hard on them since Don split," she answered.

"Any hope of reconciliation?"

"No, I don't even know where he is. My mom's been doing a great job, but dealing with twin four-year-olds is tough when you're sixty-eight."

"Any other family around to help?"

"I'm an only child, so it's just me and my mom. Dad died a few years ago."

"Let me know if there's anything my wife and I can do to help."

"Thanks, Captain, I will," replied Hearn, ending the conversation for the moment.

Concord was now 4,000 yards away from the opening through the Chesapeake Bridge-Tunnel. There was a myriad of small boats in the area to watch out for and, moving at fifteen knots, *Concord* would be through the opening in four minutes.

On the main deck crewmembers patrolled with loaded weapons while down below others were finishing last-minute packing or donning their dress-white uniforms prior to manning the rail for entering port. Six thirty-foot Navy security boats, each with a four-man crew and mounting two machine guns, designated Papa 1 through 6, wove a protective pattern around *Concord*. Overhead an Air Cobra attack helicopter circled. Further out a local television station helicopter kept pace, its crew filming *Concord*'s return for the evening news.

"Bridge, Lookout."

"Bridge, aye," replied Lieutenant Pete Spectle, the Junior Officer of the Deck.

"Bridge, I got what looks to be a boat on fire, two people onboard, bearing zero-nine-zero, range one thousand yards."

"Bridge aye," acknowledged Spectle. Wallace, overhearing the report, issued the orders: "Have Papa six investigate and send a MAYDAY to the Coast Guard on channel sixteen."

"Aye, aye, Captain."

Picking up a radio handset, and using *Concord*'s tactical call sign "Minuteman," Spectle radioed the instructions to Papa 6, patrolling astern of *Concord*. As the boat peeled off at high speed in response to the order, the lookout called:

"Bridge, there are two speedboats bearing three-four-zero and two speedboats bearing zero-two-zero off the bow, range to all four boats approximately two thousand yards and closing."

Spectle again acknowledged the report: "Lookout, Bridge. Roger, we see them."

He relayed the report to the captain.

"Pass the info to Papa One and Papa Two and have them intercept," ordered Wallace.

"Aye, aye, Captain," responded Spectle. "Papa one, Papa two, this is Minuteman, over."

"Minuteman, this is Papa One, over."

"Papa one, be advised there are four, repeat four speed boats on our bow, two to port, two to starboard, range approximately two thousands yards. Intercept and report. Over."

"Roger," Papa I answered, and then radioed, "Papa Two, take the two to starboard. I'll cover the two to port." Papa 1 and 2 increased speed and headed for the contacts while Papa 3 and Papa 4 moved from their positions to cover the now-exposed area ahead of the cruiser.

As Papa 1 approached the intruders, one of her crew yelled, "Will you look at this!" Each speedboat had a gorgeous bikini-clad brunette standing up in the bow, waving a "Welcome Home" banner.

"Minuteman, this is Papa Two. The contacts look like a welcoming committee."

"Papa Two, roger, move them out of the zone."

"With pleasure. Out."

With most of the attention focused on Papa 1 and 2, Wallace focused on Papa 6. Through his binoculars he saw Papa 6 pull alongside the burning pleasure boat.

"Oh my God," he whispered as the burning boat exploded, obliterating itself and Papa 6.

"Spectle, order Papa Five and Hawk One to head for the scene and sound the Rescue and Assistance alarm."

Overhead the Air Cobra, with Papa 5 following, headed for the smoke and flotsam marking the remains of Papa 6.

With most of the ship's crew preparing to deal with the disaster astern, Papa 1 and Papa 2 moved toward the four speed boats off the bow. On board *Concord*, the Bridge Watch monitored the operations. After getting a good look at the incoming boats, Wallace told Hearn, "Looks like they have it under control."

Closing the last hundred feet to their respective targets, weapons ready, the Papa crews tensed as the girls reached down and brought up brightly-colored water guns.

"Don't shoot!" the Navy gunners called out to their mates, "they're super-soaker water guns." Everybody relaxed.

Seeing the water guns, Spectle muttered, "Looks like somebody's idea of a joke."

When the smiling women fired, bullets from their disguised AK-47s ripped the Navy crews to shreds. After eliminating the closest security boats, the intruders' guns turned first on the two remaining security boats, then the cruiser.

Dashing to the IMC, the ship's public-address system, Wallace yelled, "Deck Security, open fire, repeat, open fire. All hands, man your Battle Stations. Set Condition Zebra." The last meant all doors and hatches were to be closed, turning the hull into a series of watertight compartments.

Blood ran down *Concord*'s sides as the attackers' fire tore into her crew. A ragged cheer went up when defensive fire killed one of the bikini-clad terrorists. The cheering stopped as the boat kept heading straight for *Concord*'s bow. Zigzagging, the other three boats drove on, their hulls splintered, the women gunners dead, but the helmsmen were safe behind armor-plated consoles.

Harry "Slick" Jones, coxswain of Papa 4, was dying; the rest of his crew was already dead. "Just one," Jones prayed. "Just let me take one of the bastards with me."

The fourth attacker had swung wide, apparently heading for *Concord*'s stern. Using skills honed by a lifetime on the water, Jones instantly calculated an intercept point. The enemy coxswain didn't see Papa 4 approaching until it was too late. Screaming "So long, mother-fucker!" Jones rammed the speedboat's side, triggering an explosion which pulverized the two craft.

CHOKE POINTS

The explosion rocked *Concord*, and before anyone could recover, the remaining three boats, each loaded with explosives, crashed into the cruiser's hull and detonated, catapulting people into steel walls, crushing limbs and lives. The blast blew the bridge windows inward; screams and black smoke wafted upward. A piece of glass ripped open Debra Hearn's throat, showering Wallace with blood. The helmsman's legs were shattered, the bones sticking out from tattered trousers. Others were dazed, wounded or unconscious.

Groping his way to the intercom, Wallace called: "Damage Control, this is the Bridge. Report." Waiting for the reply, he tried to wipe Hearn's blood from his eyes and face.

The team at Damage Control Central, buried in the bowels of the ship, had been badly shaken, but was still functioning. Commander Juan Ramirez, the Executive Officer, scanned the status boards by the light of battery-powered battle lanterns and listened to reports pouring in from the Damage Control parties investigating interior spaces. The news was all bad. Fires from electrical short circuits and ruptured fuel lines raged unchecked. Ladders were down, blocking passageways; jammed hatches prevented access to spaces, trapping many of the crew below decks. In the darkness the survivors crawled on hands and knees, looking for ways out that no longer existed.

"Captain, there's a fifteen-foot hole in the port bow, and a twenty-by-ten gash amidships starboard side," Ramirez reported. "One explosive smashed the stern, opening it to the sea. We've lost power. No report from the engine room watch; they're probably dead from the explosion. No report on casualties yet. It's too soon to accurately count the dead and wounded," he concluded.

Concord's momentum kept her moving forward, toward the opening between spans of the Chesapeake Bay Bridge Tunnel. Water surging into the hole in the bow pulled *Concord* to port, and the incoming tide pushed the ship's stern broadside across the channel. Wallace watched helplessly as the ship heeled to port and started sinking in the opening. Feeling a hand on his shoulder, he turned to see Pete Spectle standing beside him.

"Mr. Spectle, order all hands to abandon ship," he said softly, knowing nothing more could be done for *Concord*.

Seattle, Washington, 10:00 AM (1:00PM Eastern Time)

Ellen and Bob had saved for years to take a cruise along the Inland Passage to Alaska so they could spend several leisurely months touring the state. With a first-class cabin on *Polaris Queen* and months together without distractions, it was the trip of a lifetime.

"Oh, Bob, what a view," said Ellen. "This whole trip is so exciting."

Bob hugged her. In his eyes she was as lovely as when he had married her thirty-five years ago. Having cleared Seattle Harbor, they were in Puget Sound, with Whidbey Island on their right and the small town of Nordland on the left.

Tom Vogle, the *Polar Queen*'s Master, enjoyed the scene from his vantage point on the port bridge wing. In his forty years going to sea, the *Queen*'s gleaming white hull and graceful superstructure joined to create the loveliest ship he'd commanded. Almost five hundred feet long, the ship had elegant accommodations for three hundred passengers. A crew of two hundred made sure each passenger received the finest service.

"Look at the ships, I've never seen so many," Ellen exclaimed.

Bob smiled, having seen or served on more ships than he could remember, but it was all new to Ellen. Although they had lived in many places over the years, she'd never been in anything bigger than a row boat.

"See that big fishing boat coming towards us?" she asked. "It looks like you could almost reach out and touch it."

Bob looked at the one Ellen was pointing to. The boat had a blue hull and was about seventy-five feet long, her name *Orca* painted on the bow. He saw several men on her deck and what appeared to be several lengths of pipe lying at their feet. Two more men were in the raised conning station. Everything looked normal except for two long, canvas-covered pieces of equipment mounted beside them. A black Zodiac with an outboard engine was tied to the stern.

On *Polaris Queen*'s bridge, First Officer Steve Oakley recognized the fishing boat and asked: "What's Harry doing? He knows to stay clear."

His thoughts interrupted, Vogle scanned the approaching vessel through his binoculars, but didn't see anything unusual. "Give him a call and see what's going on," Vogle said, "and tell him to get the hell away from us."

Oakley tried twice to call *Orca* over the radio, but got no response. By the time he put the handset down and headed out on the bridge wing to talk to Vogle, the fishing boat was only a few hundred yards away and closing.

"What does that idiot think he's doing?" growled Vogle. "Call the Coast Guard and see if they can reach him." To one of the men on watch, he said, "Sound the five short-blast Danger Signal on the whistle."

As the last whistle blast ended, an explosion split the bridge apart.

Also watching the approaching vessel, Bob saw one of the men on deck lift a piece of pipe to his shoulder. Comprehension came immediately. He yanked Ellen back from the rail, and shoved her down onto the deck, yelling, "Get down, get down!" to the other passengers just as the rocket-propelled grenade hit the bridge.

"Stay here and stay down," he said to Ellen. Seeing his wife was safe, Bob crawled back to the rail, and, taking cover behind a small winch, looked over the side. The canvas covering the equipment on the conning station had been removed, revealing heavy machine guns.

The men manning the guns raked the *Polaris Queen* while those on deck fired RPGs into the hull. Bullets ricocheted off the metal, creating a lethal storm of flesh-shredding shrapnel, turning the decks into a charnel house. Each RPG punctured the ship's thin sides, forming a miniature hell when it exploded.

Suddenly the firing stopped. Amid cries for help and smoky flames from burning fuel tanks in the lifeboats, Bob turned to see Ellen lying face down next to him, her head and blouse bloody. Terrified of being left alone, she had crawled up behind him.

With gentle, well-practiced hands, he examined her. The head wound was only a scratch, messy, but not dangerous. Moving down, he didn't find any wounds in her back, so he turned her over. A ricochet had sliced diagonally from Ellen's right shoulder to left hip, opening her entire chest and stomach. There was nothing he could do.

"It's not your fault," she whispered, and with a brief smile, died.

CHOKE POINTS

His eyes filled with grief and tears, Bob bent over and kissed her still warm lips. Then he stood up, stiff with rage. For the first time in memory, he was without a weapon and helpless to strike back. Bob walked to the rail once more, hoping for a glimpse of the rogue boat. What he saw shocked him more than the attack. Instead of speeding away, *Orca* had turned around and was coming back. There was no firing this time. Bob saw six people calmly boarding the Zodiac, one starting the engine and heading them for the nearest shore. His last memory was the abandoned fishing boat smashing into the *Polaris Queen*'s stern with an incendiary flash.

PART I

YEARS

01

**Baghdad
March 2003**

Under Saddam Hussein, the Iraqi security structure known as *Al-Mukhabarat al-'Iraqiyya* (The Iraqi Mukhabarat, commonly referred to as the *Mukhabarat*) was made up of five primary agencies: the *al-Amn al-Khas* (Special Security), *al-Amn al-'Amm* (General Security), *al-Mukhabarat* (General Intelligence), *al-Istikhbarat* (Military Intelligence) and *al-Amn al-'Askari* (Military Security). In addition, there was a myriad of Ba'ath Party security agencies, civil police forces, paramilitary militias, and special military units which protected the regime.

In addition to preventing coups and protecting Saddam, these agencies, whose duties significantly and intentionally overlapped, maintained internal domestic security and conducted foreign operations. These intelligence agencies, along with the Ba'ath Party organizations and select units of the military, formed Saddam's security network, permeating every aspect of Iraqi life and ensuring his total control over the state.

Roughly, the responsibilities of *al-Amn al-Khas* (Special Security) broke down as follows: 1) provide security for the president at all times, especially during travel and public meetings; 2) secure all presidential facilities, such as palaces and offices; 3) supervise other security and intelligence services; 4) monitor government ministries and the leadership of the armed forces; 5) supervise internal security operations against the Kurdish and Shi'a opposition; 6) purchase foreign arms and technology; 7) secure Iraq's most critical military industries; and 8) direct efforts to conceal Iraq's weapons of mass destruction (WMD) programs.

While its primary duty was protecting the president, it managed the actions of the Republican Guard and the Special Republican Guard, making Special Security the regime's most important and powerful security agency.

Special Security watched over the activities of Military Intelligence and the Soviet secret police advisors [Komityet Gosudarstvennoy Bezopasnosti (KGB)] in Iraq during the 1980s as they assisted their Iraqi counterparts in concealing covert weapons production facilities. It served as the central coordinating body between Military-Industrial Commission, Military Intelligence, General Intelligence, and the military in the covert procurement of the necessary components for Iraq's weapons of mass destruction.

During the 1991 Gulf War, it was put in charge of concealing SCUD missiles, and afterwards, handled the movement and concealment of key documents from the United Nations Special Commission (UNSCOM) inspections, relating to Iraq's weapons programs. It is also thought that Special Security was responsible for commercial trade conducted covertly in violation of UN sanctions, especially with Iran.

Located on a street lined with mansions belonging to such high-ranking members of Iraq's power structure as Hussein's son Odai, the Mukhabarat building was a sprawling, four-story mansion with no sign indicating its purpose, and its location was not known to the general public. The spy agency's main headquarters building was about two miles away in the Mansour district on the other side of the Tigris River.

Al-Mukhabarat al-'Iraqiyya (Iraqi Intelligence Headquarters Office of *al-Amn al-Khas* (Special Security)

Heavy drapes across the windows muted the sound of the armored personnel carriers and trucks laden with troops in the street below. In his office, Colonel Quhir Nabi-Ulmalhamsh al-Hishma poured two glasses of chilled vodka. Handing one to Pytor Ivanov Demivov, the colonel seated himself on the opposite side of the gold inlaid coffee table.

"Cheers, Pytor!"

"*Za vashe zdorovye*," replied Demivov before downing the vodka in one swallow. He poured another drink for each of them and lit a Marlboro cigarette. Inhaling deeply he let the smoke trickle out through his nose.

"Well, my Russian friend, the Americans will be here shortly."

"They won't find anything interesting—all the material is in Syria. You were wise to work with me on that. The convoys didn't attract any attention and my associates on the other end have already dispersed the most valuable weapons and materials to discrete locations in Europe."

During the previous weeks, Soviet *Spetsnaz* special-operations forces, operating under the authority of the military intelligence service [Glavnoje Razvedyvatel'noje Upravlenije (GRU)], organized large commercial truck convoys which moved many of Saddam Hussein's weapons and related goods out of Iraq.

The weapons included missile components, MiG jet parts, tank parts, chemicals used to make chemical weapons, high explosives, and related technology—from some 200 arms depots was systematically separated from the inventory of conventional weapons and sent to Syria, Lebanon, and, possibly, Iran. The material included 194.7 metric tons of HMX, or high-melting-point explosive; 141.2 metric tons of RDX, or rapid-detonation explosive; and 5.8 metric tons of PETN (pentaerythritol tetranitrate), all of which are used to manufacture "plastic" high-explosive and nuclear weapons.

The Iraqi government paid the Kremlin for the Special Forces to provide security for Iraq's Russian arms and to conduct counterintelligence activities designed to prevent U.S. and Western intelligence services from learning about the arms pipeline through Syria. The withdrawal of Russian-made weapons and explosives from Iraq was part of a plan by Saddam to set up a facility in Syria that could be used for launching pro-Saddam insurgency operations in Iraq, should the need arise.

The colonel smiled. "It will be valuable to the right parties. Your contacts once again proved worthwhile, just as they did during the West's Oil-for-Food fiasco. It was very profitable for us all."

The United Nations Security Council adopted the Oil-for-Food Program in 1995 after widespread criticism of the humanitarian crisis in Iraq under comprehensive economic sanctions. After delays, humanitarian supplies began to arrive in 1997. Though the program lessened the crisis, it did not end it. Under its rules, the UN controlled all revenues from Iraq's oil sales, and contracts within the program were subject to oversight. The US and the UK often imposed political blockages on legitimate humanitarian contracts, claiming "dual-use" as military items. Procedures were slow, monies were withheld for war reparations, and Iraq's oil industry could not obtain either investments or adequate spare parts. Beginning in late 2001, the US-UK throttled Iraq's oil sales through abusive control over the contract price, drastically reducing funds available for the program. The adoption of Resolution 1483 in May 2003 put an end to sanctions, and foresaw the phasing out of the program over six months and the gradual transfer of its administration to the US-UK authorities in Iraq.

Changing the subject al-Hishma asked: "Are the conventional weapons and mines on their way?"

"Yes, three small freighters and a large tanker passed through the blockade three nights ago," replied Demivov with a thin smile. "Valuable cargo for our friends. Your part will be deposited as usual."

Al-Hishma returned the smile. In addition to the money from selling surplus Iraqi weapons to anyone who could afford them, he had cleared fifty million dollars during the Oil-for-Food Program. It had been easy. The colonel received kickbacks from the shipping lines contracted to carry the oil, monies from the sale of the oil to brokers, and bribes from the companies who wished access to the cheap oil through those same brokers.

Demivov sat back, lighting another cigarette from the stub of the first one. "What are your plans after the Americans come?"

"Slip into Bahrain and set up shop there. It is an unlikely place to work from and is easily accessible for anyone I need to see. There are several front companies already in place, so the groundwork has been laid for my arrival. Before that happens, I plan to oversee the destruction of a covert American operation on the coast." He was almost smirking by this point.. "And you?"

"There's an opening for me in Washington. One of our agents is having trouble with an official in the Administration. I am to smooth out the trouble."

Al-Hishma nodded. "We'll stay in touch through the usual means. There is still much business to be done."

The two men toasted each other with another round of vodka standing and shaking hands.

"I wish you well in the heart of infidel territory," al-Hishma offered as the Russian headed for the door.

"May all your ventures be successful," returned Demivov.

02

March 2003

US Naval Special Warfare (NSW) played a significant role in Operation Iraqi Freedom, employing the largest number of SEALs and Special Warfare Combat Craft Crewmen (SWCC) in its history. NSW forces were instrumental in the success of initial special-reconnaissance and direct-action missions, including the securing of the southern oil infrastructures of the Al Faw peninsula and the off-shore gas and oil terminals (GOPLATS); the clearing of the Khor Al Abdullah and Khor Az Zubayar waterways that enabled the first humanitarian aid to be delivered to the vital port city of Umm Qasr; reconnaissance of the Shat Al Arab waterway; capture of high-value targets; raids on suspected chemical, biological and radiological sites; and classified/covert operations. Stretched too thinly to meet all of the tasks, a number of non-special assets were employed.

Off the Coast of Iraq

"Of all the idiotic, squat-for-brains things you've done, this takes the cake. Why in the world did you agree to run a rubber boat with seven snake-eating SEALs into a place where there's a real good chance of getting your butt shot off?" thought Mark James Fletcher as they headed toward the beach.

Fletcher's latest adventure had started three days earlier when a eight-man Navy SEAL team came aboard Fletcher's ship, the 378-foot Coast Guard cutter USCGC *Evans*. The team's mission was to seize one of the Iraqi-controlled offshore oil rigs.

Special Operations Chief (SOC) Chief Bob Davies, in charge of the team, asked for a volunteer to handle the boat taking the team to its target. As a mustang lieutenant and the most experienced coxswain on *Evans*, Fletcher volunteered.

The mission proved to be anti-climatic: The tower was unoccupied. The only casualty was the broken ankle one of the team suffered jumping from the boat to the tower. Two days later Fletcher was summoned to the commanding officer's cabin. After complimenting Fletcher on his work with the SEALs, the CO wasted no time.

"I have a message from Navy headquarters instructing me to send you TAD (temporary Additional Duty) to the Navy for the next four days. In two hours, a small boat will take you ashore and you'll be met on the dock with further instructions. If anybody on board asks, tell them you've been granted a ninety-six-hour liberty."

Stunned, Fletcher asked: "What's going on?"

The CO snapped, "I don't know and when I asked, I was told I don't need to know." In a gentler voice, he added: "Mark, I wish I knew. All I can say is good luck and take care of yourself. I'll see you in four days."

SEAL Headquarters

Lieutenant Luke Robichaud was trying to figure out how he was going to handle two critical missions with one SEAL platoon. His headquarters consisted of a bare room with two battered desks, three folding chairs, two phones and no air-conditioning. The good news was he had a new laptop computer to work with. The bad news was that it provided a means for his superiors to send him orders he didn't want to deal with.

The SEAL teams were stretched to the max, and Robichaud told his superiors that one team was down a man, but no one at CENTCOM seemed to care.

CHOKE POINTS

"Excuse me," a voice said, breaking Robichaud's concentration.

Annoyed, he looked up and saw a sweat-soaked figure standing in the office door. Robichaud barked: "What do you want?"

"I'm LTJG Mark Fletcher, Coast Guard. I'm TAD from the CGC *Evans* and was told to report to this building," replied Fletcher to the jeans and polo shirt clad questioner. "Who are you?"

"I'm Lieutenant Luke Robichaud. Does that answer your question?" Ignoring the surprised look on Fletcher's face, Robichaud picked up one of the phones and punched in a number. "Chief Davies, the Coast Guard's arrived." Putting down the phone he told Fletcher to sit down.

A few minutes later there was a knock on the door. "Chief Davies reporting as ordered, sir."

Fletcher looked up. "Hi, Chief, what's going on?"

Robichaud intervened, using the same hard-assed tone, before Davies could respond. "Fletcher, everything you hear or see from now on is classified Top Secret. If you shoot your mouth off, I'll hear about it—and that's not something you want to have happen. Understand?"

"Yes, sir."

"We've been tasked to exfiltrate an Iraqi intelligence officer and land additional equipment for another operation," Robichaud began. "Because the chief's team is down a man, so they need someone to handle the boat, and the chief recommended you. That's it. Are you willing to go?"

Without hesitation, Fletcher answered: "Yes, sir."

Robichaud smiled and shook his head. "Chief, he's yours, but bring him back in one piece or you can kiss your ass goodbye."

"Aye-aye, sir. Okay, LT, let's go"

SEAL Team Hut

As they opened the door, seven pairs of eyes turned to see who was invading their space.

"We're good to go," announced Davies. "The LT gave his blessing for Fletcher to come along."

Fletcher scoped out the hut. Around the walls were eight bunks with a small table and a lamp by each bunk, shelves for personal gear, a couple of easy chairs, and a small refrigerator. In the center, six chairs surrounded a table made from a packing crate, its top bare except for a few magazines and Louis L'Amour westerns. Best of all, an air conditioner labored in the window.

"Now that you're here, let me introduce you to the team," offered Davies. "The wiry Cajon is Jean-Paul La Beque, known as Gator. The big ugly mother next to you is Chris Jones, aka Web; the little ugly mother next to him is Julio Sanchez, who goes by Rico. Sprawled in the chairs are Jim Grim whose handle is Reaper, Dick Spencer, and Vic Patton. And the gimp on crutches is our surfer, Doug Sandman. And, from now on, call me Go-Go."

"Okay, Go-Go, what's the mission?"

"As the LT told you, we're to exfiltrate a High Value Target and provide additional secure communications gear to another member of his cell. Five days ago we did a recon of the area and marked channels through the minefields. We'll be dropped three klicks off the beach, make our run, drop the stuff, and head home. It's your basic KISS operation," answered Davies.

"So it's a covert beach party without the girls or beer."

Everybody laughed.

"That's one way to put. I'll buy the beer when we get back, but you have to supply your own girl," replied Go-Go, before snapping orders out. "Gator, get him some cammies, body armor, and a weapon. While Gator's doing that, get your check ride in the boat. "

The boat turned out to be a FC470 combat rubber raiding craft (CRRC) fifteen-foot, six-inch long ridged hull inflatable (RHIB) powered by a fifty-five horse-power MARS outboard motor. After giving the outboard a thorough going-over, they got underway.

Three hours later they headed back to the hut. Davies, Web, and Gator were going over equipment and weapons when the trio came in.

"The boat's ready to go, but the motor's too noisy," said Mark as he flopped into a chair after grabbing a bottle of water from the refrigerator.

"Well, we can't paddle it and it's too late to find other transportation. Got any suggestions?" said Davies.

"Yeah, I do. We fit PVC tubing to the exhaust pipes and extend them below the water, which eliminate most of the noise from the motor. Also, we wrap the muffler in a blanket. It shouldn't take too long to put together," answered Mark.

"Where'd you get that idea?" asked Rico.

"I read a lot," Mark replied, "and Fredrick Forsyth used that trick in his book *Dogs of War*. My bet is he learned it from the mercenaries he knew."

After thinking about it, Davies said, "Sounds good, let's try it. Web, you and Sandman take care of it. " Turning back to Mark, he continued: "Your gear's here, so let's get you fitted up."

It consisted of a Special Operations Forces personal equipment advanced requirements (SPEAR) modular/integrated communications helmet (MICH) with PVS-15 dual tube night vision binocular system mounted on the front, SPEAR body armor, and a M11 Sig Sauer 9 mm pistol.

"It all looks good, Go-Go, but I brought my own pistol."

"Okay, let's see it."

Fletcher unzipped his bag and took out a canvas-wrapped bundle. Inside was a well-worn web belt with a leather military-style holster clipped to it. The holster's top flap had been cut off, revealing a Model 1911A1 .45 caliber pistol, the type Americans had carried through four wars.

On the grip was an intricately-carved Marine Corps anchor-and-globe emblem. Also attached to the belt were a K-bar knife and a pouch holding two spare magazines for the pistol. Fletcher took the pistol out of its holster, popped the magazine out of the handle and pulled the slide back, locking it in the open position. That done, he handed it, butt first, to Bob.

Davies carefully examined the pistol. It was in beautiful shape. He noticed on the other side of the grip were carved the words SEMPER FI and the date 4 APRIL 1945. "Where'd you get this?"

"It's my grandfather's from World War II in the Pacific," said Fletcher. "My dad carried it in Vietnam. He gave it to me the night before I deployed over here. My great uncle was in WWII, the K-bar is his. They said I might find them useful."

"They were right, but can you hit anything with it?" Davies said, returning the pistol. "Now get some rest, the final briefing is at 1800."

03

0300
Off the Coast of Iraq

Clouds obscured the late rising moon and the sultry air lay heavy around them. Gator felt the boat slow down, the signal that it was time to go for a swim. He, Web, Grim, and Rico had the point, going ashore ahead of the rest of the team as scout swimmers to insure there were no surprises waiting for them. Donning fins and masks, they shouldered their weapons bags and slipped over the side. They stopped in the surf line to scan the beach before going ashore. The beach sloped gently upward for about twenty meters to a ridge before leveling off to the coast highway, two hundred meters further inland.

As they came out of the surf, Rico went right while Gator headed left up the slope to the ridge. Web and Grim with M-60 machines guns moved to cover the corners of the landing zone. Neither Rico nor Gator saw or heard anything. After completing a diamond recon, Rico reported to Davies that the beach was clear. After receiving broke squelch twice in acknowledgement, Rico settled down behind some low scrub just below the seaward side of the ridge, with Gator twenty meters off to his left. Web and Reaper moved inland, positioning themselves at the far corners of the zone. Nothing blocked their vision in any direction. Contact was 0300, half an hour away, with the rest of the team coming in at 0255. It was going to be a long, lonely twenty-five minutes.

Davies heard Rico's signal and relaxed a little. Maybe, just maybe, it would go as planned, but it paid to believe otherwise. He looked around, noticing Patton checking his weapons for the umpteenth time while Fletcher calmly worked to keep the boat in position. "I made a good call bringing Fletcher along," he thought, "but we're not done yet."

On the beach, Gator also heard the "all clear" message. In addition to the CAR-15 rifle and a 9mm pistol, he carried a 12-gauge pump RAM 870 shotgun loaded with buckshot. As far as he was concerned, nothing beat it for close-in work.

At 0250, Mark felt a tap on his arm and looked up to see Davies pointing towards the beach. It was time to go.

Gator carefully scanned the highway, trying to ignore the bugs crawling down his back. It was something he'd never get used to. A shower and a cold beer when they got back were going to feel real good. A few minutes later he heard the low buzz of the outboard, followed by a soft scrunch as the boat landed. Taking a quick look to be sure Rico had heard it too, Gator headed down to help unload the supplies. As he reached the water, Fletcher was thrusting a spike with a line attached into the sand. The other end was tied to the bow of the boat.

Fletcher watched as Gator easily hefted one of the fifty-pound containers of supplies and head back up the slope. Davies grabbed another and Web took a third. As planned, Spencer and Patton helped Fletcher turn the boat around, then stood by the boat.

If all went well, the team would be clear in about fifteen minutes. Fletcher was conscious of the pistol on his hip with its load of eight rounds. His father taught him to always have a round in the chamber in addition to the seven in the magazine.

At 0300 the SEALs along the ridge saw twin pinpoints of light coming down the highway before they heard the sound of the truck's engine. It stopped opposite their position and someone got out of the cab, someone smart enough to insure no light came on when he opened the door. After stretching and looking around, there were two brief flickers of light, like a man trying to light a cigarette and the wind blowing out the matches. After Davies flashed the countersign, the figure walked to meet the SEALs.

"This guy's pretty good, looks like we're dealing with a professional for a change," whispered Davies to the others.

"You have the supplies?" the figure asked as he reached Davies.

"Yeah, but we aren't hauling them to the truck for you."

Turning back to face the truck, the man said, "No problem, as you Americans say. I've brought my own help."

Bringing a radio to his lips, he spoke into it briefly. Figures began jumping from the back of the truck, spreading out as they headed toward the waiting men.

"Isn't this beach supposed to be mined?" asked Gator of no one in particular. "They should be coming up single file." Then it hit him.

"Ambush!" he yelled, opening fire on the figures coming from the road.

Davies heard the shout and gunfire; something struck him hard in the ribs. The man he'd been talking with had stabbed him, but Davies' body armor deflected the blow. Reflexively blocking the next thrust with his left arm, he snapped his assailant's head back with the heel of his right hand. The man fell hard, out of the fight. Dropping to the ground, with bullets kicking up the sand around him, Davies checked on his men. Rico was firing, but there was blood on his leg; Web seemed to be okay; and Gator was shooting left-handed, his right arm pressed against his ribs.

A machine gun mounted in the back of the truck swept the ridgeline while the assault team moved up the flanks. Web and Grim swept the assault team with streams of machine-gun fire. Getting Web's attention, Davies pointed to the truck. Web nodded, immediately adding his fire to the chief's.

When the shooting started, Mark started toward the ridge, but stopped after a couple of strides. The team wasn't expecting anybody to come up behind them, so they'd probably shoot first and sort it out later. And, just as significant, Mark was the boat driver, so he headed back, ready to provide covering fire if necessary.

Rico was in pain; the initial shock had worn off and his leg was on fire. "Later," he thought, "I'll worry about it later." Men were closing in on the right, teams of two, leap-frogging toward the ridge; one team covered while the next moved forward. Pulling the pin from a grenade and flipping up the lever, Rico did a slow count to three and threw it at the closest team. The screams accompanying the explosion were music to his ears. He lofted more grenades down range. Just as he released the last one, his hand went numb; a bullet had hit his arm, breaking the bone as it passed through.

Web and Grim started back to the waterline, firing as they went. Their PVS-15 night vision goggles enabled them to distinguish friend from foe by the infra-red flags on the SEALs' shoulders.

Rico was trying to knock out the machine gun as Gator lay next to him, keeping the bad guys away. The truck's gas tank blew with a *whoomph*, flames lighting up the sky. Gator stopped firing. Rico looked down to see him trying to reload his M4 submachine gun one-handed, his right side bloody.

Slamming a new magazine into his own weapon, he handed it to Gator, taking the empty one. He was reaching for a fresh magazine when three figures came out of nowhere. Dropping the useless weapon, Rico flipped up his shotgun and fired, catching the first man full in the face. Swinging to his right as he pumped another round into the chamber, he pulled the trigger, opening that attacker's chest to the night air. On Rico's left side, the third assailant was too close to get a good shot at. Continuing to swing to his right, he drove the butt of the shotgun into the last man's gut and then fired into the prone figure to make sure of the kill.

When the truck blew, Davies concentrated on the remaining enemy in his sector. Until they were dealt with, it was too dangerous to pull back to the boat. He knew from the sounds of their weapons that Gator and Web were still in business, but he hadn't heard anything coming from Rico's position after the grenades exploded. Looking over, he saw a blood-covered figure trying to wrap a bandage around his arm. Sensing movement out of the corner of his eye, Davies turned, ripped off a three-round burst, shifted left, fired three more rounds, and back to the right with a final three rounds. The sound of bullets hitting flesh was followed by silence. There was no more movement.

Shoving a fresh magazine into his weapon, he called: "Let's get out of here before re-enforcements show up." He scooped

Gator up over his shoulder in a fireman's carry and headed for the shoreline, stopping halfway to cover Rico. Once Web, Grim, and Rico got to the boat, Davies finished the trip.

Fletcher saw the men coming down the slope. Soon Spencer was getting Gator, who was grunting in pain, into the boat. Web had just taken him from Davies when a bullet struck Davies in the back.

As Mark sighted on the flame-silhouetted figure, a bullet grazed his left shoulder. Ignoring the pain, he centered the sights and squeezed the trigger. A miss. The devil was still standing. Fletcher brought the muzzle down and fired again. Hit. The heavy slug lifted the shooter off the ground and flung it into the flames.

04

October 2007
Seef, Bahrain

A silver Mercedes SL600 eased out of the heavy Shaikh Khalifa Bin Salman Highway traffic onto Avenue 40, and turned right into the parking garage adjacent to the newest office building. Finding a spot in one of the far corners, the driver got out and stretched, turning in a full circle as he did so. Although most of the garage was within range of security cameras, none appeared to cover this particular area. Taking a PDA out of his sport-jacket pocket, and keeping his head lowered toward the screen, he walked to the elevators.

The reception area of Gulf Import Export, LLC was pleasantly cool with soft background music mixing with the aroma of sandalwood. In contrast to the expensive Scandinavian décor, the receptionist was wearing a burqa which hid all but her slim hands and a pair of sea-green eyes.

In accented English, she asked: "May I help you?"

"I'm here to see Ghassan al Akbar."

"He is quite busy. Do you have an appointment?"

"No, but please take him this," he said, placing a pack of Marlboro cigarettes on the receptionist's desk. "See if he can find the time."

She picked up the pack and soundlessly opened the door behind her. Returning within a minute, she gestured for the visitor to enter and closed the door behind him.

The sumptuous inner office was adorned with the finest antique furniture and Persian carpets. The windows faced northeast, overlooking the gulf. Along one wall, a couch and three comfortable chairs surrounded a gold-inlaid coffee table. On the table stood glasses and a chilled bottle of vodka.

"I see you're still smoking American cigarettes, Pytor."

"And you haven't lost your taste for fine furniture, Colonel."

Former Colonel Quhir Nabi-Ulmalhamsh al-Hishma of the Iraqi Special Security Department poured two glasses of vodka. After handing one to Pytor Ivanov Demivov, the colonel seated himself on the couch while the Russian settled into one of the chairs. Wordlessly, they raised their glasses to each other before draining them. After he refilled the glasses, Demivov lit a cigarette.

"After more than four years, why have you sought me out, Pytor?" The polite moment was over.

"Are you still interested in driving the Americans out of Iraq?" Demivov countered.

"Of course. Did you come only to pose an ignorant question?" snapped the colonel. "Or to remind me of an intolerable situation we have not, as yet, been able to remedy?"

"No, I just wanted to make sure you hadn't lost your hatred of those particular infidels along with the use of your arm," replied the Russian.

Emotions stirred by the verbal attack, Al-Hishma fought to hide his agitation. To buy some time, he drank his vodka, and, once more in control of his emotions, he asked again:

"Did you come only to pose an ignorant question, or to remind me of an intolerable situation we have not, as yet, been able to remedy?"

"No, I have come for neither. And there is a simple way to force all unwanted foreign troops out and put the Baathists back in control."

CHOKE POINTS

Al-Hishma raised an eyebrow. "How do you propose to do what no one else has been able to do?"

"Cut off their supplies at the source. Remember the saying 'amateurs talk tactics, professionals study logistics'?"

"Brilliant!" the colonel sneered. "What do we do? Use our nonexistent weapons of mass destruction on their cities? You've lost your mind. And, supposing we can do the impossible, how do we then dispose of the opposition within Iraq?"

Knowing he had the colonel hooked, Demivov said, "In answer to your second question, my sponsors control the transportation of weapons to all factions in Iraq. This is easy, since, as you know, the weapons all come from the three major suppliers. Once the Americans are gone, the weapons will only go to whom you choose."

Momentarily shocked by this bit of information he had never even suspected, al-Hishma poured more vodka for himself and his guest. Taking his time, he continued, "So, since you have obviously thought that through, how do we stop the supplies? The world will not tolerate a mass murder—even if it's of Americans."

"We don't need to. Let me explain."

Listening carefully, Al-Hishma was thoroughly impressed with the plan Demivov laid out for him. It was simple, and as far as he could see, flawless.

"But why should I undertake the project, even for such a worthy goal?"

Without a word, Demivov handed over an envelope containing a single sheet of paper on which were typed seven words.

"What is this?" al-Hishma demanded after reading it. "There is nothing in here I need."

"It is the name of the man you have sought for four years, the one responsible for what you have become."

"What do your sponsors what in return?"

"Nothing you can't live with," replied Demivov, and went on to explain that part of the plan.

When he was finished, al-Hishma nodded. "I agree it is an acceptable price."

Demivov plunged into a detailed outline of the logistics, communications, personnel, and timing. The keys to success were in not using the same method twice and having their assets in place before launching the first attack. An hour later, all was in place, and Demivov got up to leave.

As he did so, al-Hishma poured one more round of vodka.

"Cheers, Pytor!"

"*Za vashe zdorovye,*" replied Demivov, echoing their last toast from four years earlier.

Reaching into his pocket, he handed the colonel a cell phone. "Use this to call me when you have the necessary details in place. We'll take care of the logistics for you."

"You'll hear from me within the month," said al-Hishma.

Satisfied the interview had gone as planned, Demivov drove east to a small restaurant he knew for dinner before catching his flight back to the States. Once settled at a shadowed table at the back of the restaurant, he ordered vodka. After it was delivered, he took out his cell phone.

New York City

In a Seiako International executive conference room overlooking New York harbor, a vibration signaling an incoming call alerted the slim, severely-tailored woman that a long-awaited message was about to be delivered.

"Excuse me, Paul," Evelyn LaBlanc said to the man who was giving a report on the company's declining revenues, "but I need to take a short break. We'll reconvene in fifteen minutes."

Paul and the others at the meeting were not pleased, but they had no choice but to sit and wait. It was, after all, her company, not theirs.

Her elegant office suite projected an aura of wealth and power. Answering the phone as the door closed, she asked: "A success?"

"Yes, he went for it without any hesitation," replied the Russian.

"And the time frame?"

"Exactly as you wanted. He'll start within the month, and wrap up the project within eight months."

"Excellent. Call me when you're back and we'll set up a meeting to discuss this further." She broke the connection. The call, lasting less than a minute, was totally untraceable—had anyone been interested in doing so. Everything was meshing perfectly. The Mexican project would be completed shortly before al-Hishma struck. Once that happened, she would achieve two goals: financial power and the death of her family's oldest enemy.

Seef, Bahrain

The burqa-clad receptionist watched as the carefully-concealed security cameras tracked Demivov to his car and then his exit from the garage. Once he was safely away, she entered al-Hishma's office without knocking, shedding the burqa as soon as the door closed behind her. Underneath the camouflaging costume, she wore a mini-shirt and flowing translucent top.

"What do you think of the visit, Gwen?" he asked, handing her a drink.

Gwen accepted it gratefully while shaking loose her long auburn hair. She settled into the chair Demivov had occupied a short time earlier before answering.

"The proposal was good, but too smooth, too smooth by a long shot. What was in the note that made you agree to the project?"

Gwen had seen the interview thanks to the cameras and microphones blanketing al-Hishma's office, but had not been able to read the note.

Silently he handed it to her.

"Oh my God," she whispered after reading the few words.

He allowed himself a smug smile. "Yes. Now, let us begin to see how we can use this and the Russian to our own ends."

PART II

MONTHS

05

March 2008
Chicago, Illinois

The sun was painfully bright as the man stepped from the cab, but an unseasonably cold north wind lanced through his coat during the short walk to the building's entrance. Nodding toward the security desk, he headed for the elevators, which took him to the office of Gulf Import Export, LLC, a private firm with branches in Norfolk, Los Angeles, Galveston, and Bahrain. This office was the largest, consisting of a reception area, two small private offices and a conference room, all furnished in mid-American office chic.

As the office door opened, the auburn-haired secretary greeted him with a warm smile. Normally there were few visitors, and very few arrived without being summoned.

"If I'd studied climate as well as geography, I would have chosen somewhere warmer as a base to work from."

"The night's faxes are on your desk and the conference call with Vreeland and Lokesh is scheduled for 11:00."

"Good, when the call comes in, transfer it to my office and then join me," he replied.

In his office Allen Ryse shrugged off his coat and then scanned the messages. There was nothing new and, more importantly, nothing to be concerned about. Booting up the computer and logging in, he read the waiting e-mails. Again, there was nothing alarming in them. Donning the headset used with the interactive voice software, replies were quickly dictated and sent.

Promptly at 11:00 the phone rang. Gwen Goldin came in as he hit the speaker button.

"Status report," said Ryse without preamble.

"Vreeland here," began the associate from Virginia. "We are on schedule with the arrangements in Newark, Norfolk, New York, Texas, and Louisiana. The last of our work crews will be arriving shortly."

"Good," Ryse said. "Get the new personnel settled in, and then have them begin manning our regional offices. Once everyone is in place, begin to acquire the peripheral equipment locally."

"Agreed," replied Vreeland.

It was Lokesh's turn to report. "The timely arrival of the work force and equipment for our Seattle and California clients has also been confirmed."

"And, Lokesh, have there been any changes or new developments at your client sites?" asked Ryse.

"None."

"I ask the same question of you, Vreeland."

"Also none," said Vreeland

"Then we are finished," Ryse said, cutting the connection.

As expected Goldin did not participate in the conversation; her purpose was to listen for any subtle shifts in voice inflections or unusual hesitations in Vreeland's and Lokesh's answers.

There were none; both men appeared to be telling the truth. She said as much to Ryse and returned to her desk.

Alone once more, he took a laptop computer out of his desk; it, too, was set up with interactive voice software. Ryse logged into a different e-mail account than he had used previously, and dictated: "The project is on schedule. All the items have been received by our distributors, and the preliminary materials will be delivered to each location within the next three weeks."

After giving the send command, he shut down the unit, sat back and closed his eyes, reviewing all he'd accomplished in the six months since Demivov's visit in Bahrain.

The first order of business had been to establish a private holding company in the Belgian port of Antwerp, one of the world's largest seaports. Its purpose was two-fold: first was to shift attention away from any inference of Arab or Middle Eastern involvement in company operations. The second purpose was to provide a base within the European Union for trans-shipping the necessary weapons, explosives and ancillary equipment under false manifests, which would be lost among thousands of others passing through the port daily. To further allay any suspicion, all funds for the holding company's operations came through Belgium's largest bank.

Back in Bahrain, maps and charts; ship schedules providing arrival and departure dates for up to several years; data on potential US security countermeasures; and all available pertinent literature on each target area was assembled and studied. This was facilitated by the internet.

At that point, a thorough on-site reconnaissance of each of the targets had been undertaken. Working out of a flat in Antwerp, he or Gwen traveled to the U.S. to find reliable commercial rental agents in each of the target ports. No two trips were made to the US from the same European airport or using the same passport.

Through the rental agents, the office in Chicago had been let, as well as a combination of office and small warehouse spaces in each port. Phones, computers, and office supplies were ordered for delivery the second week in April. The necessary paperwork, forms and brochures were also put in place to insure that anyone looking into the import/export company found everything they would expect to find—and nothing else.

Another piece of the operation was applying for a US Federal Maritime Commission Ocean Transportation Intermediaries license. As an established firm in Belgium, there was no problem in obtaining the license. This, in turn, helped divert attention from the containers carrying the necessary equipment and weapons for the operation. Not that they would have drawn much interest anyway. With over ten million containers entering and leaving the U.S. annually, there was little chance of these being intercepted. To make doubly sure, the containers themselves bore no outside markings, and the manifests indicated they held household goods.

The next step was recruiting the personnel needed for each part of the operation. It was decided bringing in personnel from overseas posed less of a security risk than either using assets already in place or recruiting suitable people locally. Ryse decided he needed two subordinate mission coordinators to recruit and oversee the actual operations—one for the east coast, one for the west coast. He elected to use two men who had proven reliable in the past—although there was a slight risk they had previously been identified by western intelligence agencies. If either had refused the offered contract, Ryse would have killed him on the spot. Both accepted after being presented with a unique opportunity and the offer of two million dollars as compensation for their work.

The strain had worn Ryse down, deepening the lines on his face. Although success was just a few short weeks away, he was weary to the depth of his soul. But, as weary as he was, one thing drove him on: the need for revenge. He had been Mohamed bin Hajeed, an Iraqi intelligence officer with a brilliant future. Now, as Ryse, he was forced to work for another to achieve his purpose—power in Iraq and revenge on Lieutenant Mark Fletcher..

Seattle, Washington

Typically, it was raining when the 12:30 PM train from Vancouver pulled into the station. Among the descending passengers were three casually-dressed couples who merged into the crowd. Satisfied that no one was paying particular attention, each of the six took a different taxi to the Northgate Mall. After wandering the mall for an hour to ensure no one was following them, they met at the California Pizza Kitchen for a late lunch before separating once more, this time in pairs. One team hailed a taxi to take them to an efficiency apartment which would be home for the next two months.

At the apartment were driver's licenses, Social Security and credit cards, cash, a mix of new and second-hand clothing, and all the miscellaneous materials vital to establishing unshakable false IDs. There were also airline e-ticket confirmations for flights within the US, purchased over three weeks before to ensure no undue scrutiny from TSA agents would be triggered when they were used in the near future.

U.S—Canadian border, Vermont

"What's the purpose of your visit?" the U.S. Customs agent asked as she looked at the four sets of Canadian identification.

"We're looking forward to skiing your beautiful White Mountains," replied the driver.

While the first agent asked questions, a second one inspected the luggage and noted four sets of skis on roof racks. "How long will you be staying?"

With a smile and a wink, he said, "Only a week—but we're hoping to get snowed in." This comment brought laughs from the men and giggles from the women in the car.

"Okay, you're all set. Have a great time," finished the agent with a smile of her own.

After clearing Customs, the car resumed its journey. But, at Burlington, the car turned southeast to Boston instead of going to the ski areas.

At the same time, to the west in New York, a similar scene was playing out with another carload of six skiers, this one headed for the Adirondacks. The second continued south, stopping in Albany. In Boston and Albany, the cars were abandoned, license plates and vehicle identification numbers removed, and the keys left in the ignitions. The skis had been dumped earlier. Being late-model cars, both soon disappeared into the nether world of stolen cars and chop shops. In ones and twos over the next eight hours, the twelve skiers paid in cash for bus and train tickets to different, intermediate destinations before heading to their final one in Virginia Beach.

Leaving no paper trial, they disappeared.

Fort Lauderdale, Florida

The salt-stained forty-foot sport fishing boat mingled with the Saturday flood of boats heading in and out of the channel. Vreeland sat at the controls on the flying bridge, admiring the passing parade of bikini-clad sunbathers on the other craft. "It must be something in the water around here," he thought as a particularly luscious pair passed by.

Going across to Freeport, the Gulf Stream had been calm. Coming back was a different story. It had taken eight hours of constant battering by the notorious square waves that form when a southbound wind hits the Gulf Stream's northbound swells. In the cabin, the passengers were in rough shape, their seasickness compounded by the terror of being on the ocean. Once inside the breakwater and past any potentially curious Coast Guard or Marine Police patrol boat, the six passengers came up on deck to recuperate.

CHOKE POINTS

This would be their last sea voyage. From here on, travel would be by passenger jet or rental car. Like the team in Seattle, they, too, were taken to three different studio apartments where new IDs awaited them.

06

April 2008
Virginia Beach

The twenty-one foot center-console boat had sat in the yard on its trailer, unused, for two years. Ever since a mild stroke left him partially paralyzed, Jim hadn't been able to handle it on his own. Occasionally he'd climb aboard and sit behind the console and remember all the good times, or he'd work to keep her in good shape as he always had. But the death of his wife Martha two months before had taken the heart out of him, and he had reluctantly made a decision. A small sign sat on the trailer: FOR SALE.

On the first pleasantly warm Sunday of the spring, Jim was sitting outside on his front porch, reading the Sunday paper, when a car drove past, stopped and backed up. Jim looked up to see a young couple get out and approach him.

"Good morning, sir. I'm Pete Junger and this is my wife Sheila," said the tanned young man. "We're just out for a drive and we noticed the boat. Would you mind if we take a look at it?"

"Not at all, help yourselves."

After twenty minutes of climbing into the boat, opening lockers, peering into the bilge and inspecting the hull, they came back to the porch, and Jim invited them to sit down.

"She's in fine shape," Sheila said with a warm smile. "Why are you selling her?"

Jim briefly explained, and when he was finished, Sheila reached over and took his hand. "I'm so sorry for your loss."

"Yeah, it must be hard," Pete added. He paused for a moment. "Well, we're new to the area and have been thinking about getting a boat, but hadn't decided until we saw yours. What are you asking for it?"

Jim named his price. Pete looked at Sheila for her reaction. She nodded and gently squeezed Jim's hand.

With a smile, Pete said, "Okay, Jim, we'll take it. How about tomorrow evening we come by with the cash?"

The swiftness of the transaction and Sheila's apparent concern for him left Jim with a lump in his throat. In a husky voice he whispered, "That's fine, thanks."

After a little more small talk, Pete and Sheila said their good-byes. Once in the car and out of Jim's sight, Sheila said: "One down, three to go."

"Yeah, I hope they're all that easy," replied Pete.

Galveston, Texas

At three o'clock in the morning, high clouds partially blocked out the moon, casting shifting shadows and helping camouflage the slowly cruising boat as it neared the piers. Four divers, already in wet suits, were wearing rebreather units instead of standard scuba tanks.

Dropping off the stern, each diver took one of the underwater scooters tied to the boat's hull. Attached to each scooter was a lift bag supporting a waterproof container. Making little sound and leaving no telltale trail of bubbles, the men reached the pier unnoticed. There they carefully secured the waterproof containers for later use and returned to the boat. After getting back on board, the scooters were tied to cement blocks and pitched over the side. They wouldn't be needed again.

The operation, completed in forty-five minutes, had gone unnoticed by the container facility's security team.

Long Beach, California

Making its way up the channel with a small barge alongside, the well-used work boat was a familiar evening sight. After two months it and its crew blended into the background, completely unnoticed. Having achieved this, the real work began. Using the side of the boat next to the barge to mask their work, the crew carefully lowered a series of packages overboard and let them sink to the channel's bottom.

It took only a week to complete the mission, but the evening's runs were continued to avoid arousing suspicion.

Chicago, Illinois

It had finally warmed enough so Ryse no longer needed his overcoat, but it didn't really matter: This was his last day in the windy city.

In the office, Gwen met him with her usual warm smile. "Nothing new." She handed him a cup of coffee. "The call is set for one o'clock with Lokesh and Vreeland."

"Good. Your plans are in place for closing the office and returning to Bahrain to handle communications from the teams?"

"Yes," Gwen replied. It was a lie, she was actually going back to New York. "Then let's get this wrapped up."

The conference call with his two operatives confirmed that everything had gone smoothly in each of the target areas. No one was paying any particular attention to them and the teams' morale was high. As professionals, this was to be expected. Ryse only concern was for the groups in Virginia. Vreeland assured him they were staying within the guidelines laid out while still managing to pack as much living as possible into the time they had left.

CHOKE POINTS

Satisfied that all was going well, they reviewed timing, communications arrangements, and contingency plans. From now on, all calls would be via prepaid cell phones. This, too, was confirmed.

"You both have done well. We'll speak again in two weeks. Good hunting," said Ryse.

"Thanks, it's a pleasure working with you," Vreeland said.

Lokesh agreed and the call ended.

Picking up the cell phone Demivov had given him months ago in Bahrain, Ryse called the Russian.

It rang three times before being answered with a single word: "Da."

"We're set. The operation is on schedule."

"I wish you good hunting and look forward to the successful conclusion of our business," Demivov said and ended the call.

Gwen had listened to both calls. After the second, she entered Ryse's office carrying a tray of caviar, crackers and an ice-cold bottle of vodka. Pouring some into each of two glasses, she handed one to Ryse and curled up next to him on the couch. It would be their last time together for several weeks, and she was going to make it a memorable one for them both.

Seiako International, New York City

The ringing cell phone interrupted LaBlanc's review of the latest reports on Seiako's competitors.

"Yes?" she answered after the third ring.

Demivov said: "We're set."

"Well done. As always, it's a pleasure doing business with you."

"This is the most fun I've had in years," replied Demivov.

"I'm glad to hear that. I like a man who enjoys his work." She disconnected.

She got up and walked to the windows, reflecting on the call's significance. Five years ago, she had attempted a takeover of Terra Marine, a Hong Kong-based company that controlled 60 percent of all US port facility operations. It was done through normal business methods, and, for a number of reasons, had failed.

A better plan emerged a year later when one of her spies sent her a confidential report regarding a new megaport that was being considered. The report read in part:

> Mexico plans a multibillion-dollar project to remake Punta Colonet, a desolate, sparsely inhabited inlet two hours beyond Ensenada, into a major container port on the scale of those at Los Angeles and Long Beach. The government would turn to private companies to develop the port while giving them multi-year operating contracts. It's a system that has worked to upgrade much of the nation's infrastructure, including highways, airports, railroads and existing ports. There are substantial obstacles, among them determining how the port would be governed.
>
> The government also wants a rail line to the Mexico-California border. Other rail lines are being planned to the United States, and can move containers to Houston in the same amount of time it takes to move items from the ports of Long Beach and Los Angeles. These, in turn, will allow more economical distribution of imports to the U.S. midwest and its eastern seaboard. An airport specializing in cargo service is being discussed.
>
> Within seven years, Punta Colonet could be processing the equivalent of a million 20-foot-long containers annually, six

million by 2025. The volume predicted for Colonet is comparable to that at the ports of Los Angeles and Long Beach, which are the largest on North America's West Coast.

Global shipping companies, frustrated with backlogs at West Coast ports and especially at Long Beach and Los Angeles, are driving the project. Several appealed to the Mexican government last year to spur development of a new port in Baja California. The number of Asian cargo shipments is expanding so much that each year a new port the size of Seattle's is needed just to handle the increase.

The port and related activities are expected to spawn relatively well-paid jobs and absorb some of the migrants who continually move into Baja California. The development might promote industrial growth in other sectors, too, including aerospace, electronics and information technology.

Instead of fighting for control of US ports, it was more feasible to gain a majority interest in a new one. Working openly through Seiako, and covertly with her personal ties in Russia, China, Japan, and the Middle East, LaBlanc now had controlling interest in the project. Two of her competitors had met with unfortunate accidents, and, through holding companies, LaBlanc was able to take control of the newly leaderless shipping organizations.

The only question was how to insure the new facility was a success. The Iraqi War and Demivov provided the answer. She'd learned of al-Hishma through Demivov. Companies controlled by Seiako had arranged for a number of ships to smuggle oil out of Iraq and smuggle contraband weapons in. The Russian's ties to organized crime had also proved useful as part of the international slave trade, a business almost as profitable as weapons, and one with a larger market. Dealing with weapons and people was safer than dealing in drugs.

An unexpected bonus provided by this operation: She would also be able to destroy the last of her family's enemies.

07

May 2008
The Florida Straits
U.S. Coast Guard Cutter *Bibb*

"Sunrise is my favorite time of day at sea," mused Liz Scollins, "with the gentle surge of the ship and feeling the world wake up around you."

"Mine too," Ike Karloff agreed.

"Personally, I'd rather be sleeping," added Jeff Noonan as he turned away from the soft purple line marking the eastern horizon to check the radarscope.

The three shared the 0400 to 0800 Watch on the 270-foot U.S. Coast Guard Cutter *Bibb*. Seaman Ike Karloff was Messenger of the Watch, Seaman Elizabeth Scollins had the helm, and Lieutenant, Junior Grade Jeffrey Noonan, Officer of the Deck, had the responsibility for the safety of the entire ship.

Looking at the scope, Noonan tensed. Fifteen seconds later the other two heard him say, "Oh shit" as Noonan reached for the intercom.

"Combat, Conn," he said, two words indicating he was calling the Combat Information Center located one deck below and telling them who was calling.

"Combat, aye."

"You see what I see? Go-fast?" he asked.

"Yes, sir, we were just about to call you. The contact bears zero-three-five degrees relative, course zero-eight-five degrees true, speed thirty-five knots, range 18,000 yards, moving right to left and opening. Contact designated as Alpha. We concur that it's a drug-runner."

Noonan repeated the coordinates back, and added, "Looks like we got a live one. Good work. I'll call the captain."

"Both engines ahead full," Noonan ordered Scollins as he picked up a phone and punched a button.

It was answered immediately. "Tipper."

"Captain, this is Noonan. We have a contact evaluated as a drug-runner go-fast boat at zero-three-five relative on a course of zero-eight-five, speed thirty-five, range 18,000 going right to left and opening."

"Got it, thanks. I'm on my way up," answered Commander Jean Tipper, *Bibb*'s commanding officer. She had slept in her clothes and the feel of the engines speeding up had awaked her just before the phone buzzed.

The traditional "Captain on the Bridge" and salutes greeted Tipper when she reached the top of the ladder.

"Good morning." Karloff handed her a cup of fresh black coffee as she looked at the radarscope.

"Thanks, I appreciate this," she said, acknowledging a gesture done out of respect for her, not just her position. She turned from the radarscope to the chart table behind her.

"Let's take a look at what we have."

"Captain, we are here," Noonan said, pointing to the chart. "The closet point of land is Havana, forty miles off our starboard beam. The closest U.S. point is Key West, one hundred twenty miles north east. Our speed is nineteen knots, course zero-nine-zero; the winds are from the north at ten knots, seas calm. *Gallops Island* is fifteen miles east north east of us."

"Very well," acknowledged Tipper. "Please have the XO, operations officer, and the helo pilot report to the Bridge then set General Quarters, Intercept."

"Aye, aye, Captain," replied Noonan.

As her orders were being carried out, Tipper picked up a radio handset and pushed the transmit button. "Third base, this is Homeplate. Third base, this is Homeplate."

US Coast Guard Cutter *Gallops Island*

Lieutenant Mark Fletcher, Commanding Officer of the 110-foot Coast Guard Cutter *Gallops Island*, had taken the 0400 to 0800 Watch, partly to give the other OOD Watch Standers a break, but mostly because he enjoyed doing it. Mark glanced at the instruments to make sure everything was okay, then checked the radarscope.

A florescent blip showed up at the outer edge of the screen. He watched it for a couple of minutes then spoke to the Lookout standing nearby. "Would you go below and ask Ensign Debricko and Chief Ashton to come up?"

As the Lookout was headed down the ladder, the radio came to life.

"Third base, this Homeplate. Third base, this is Homeplate."

"Homeplate, this is Third base, go ahead," Fletcher responded, recognizing Commander Tipper's voice.

"Third base, there's a fastball heading towards you. Get ready to make the catch, we're sending Shortstop to assist. Remember to watch for any unusual spins, over."

"Roger, Homeplate, we see the fastball. Understand Shortstop assisting on the play and we are to watch for spins."

"That's affirmative. Will let you know when Shortstop is moving. Homeplate out."

The word "spins" wasn't a great code word or very original, but Fletcher knew Tipper had used it as a reminder to him. There was a rumor that instead of surrendering after being fired on by pursuing cutters or helos, the drug-runners were going to fight back, or maybe even start the fight.

"Good morning, Skipper. What's up?" said Chief Andy Ashton as he and Ed Debricko reached the Bridge, breaking Fletcher's train of thought.

"We've got a go-fast headed in our direction. *Bibb*'s launching her helo and we're closing the trap," replied Fletcher. "Ed, you're the boarding officer for this evolution. Chief, I want all weapons locked and loaded, with the gun crews wearing body armor. Both of you keep in mind the possibility that the go-fast may fire on us as we approach. Any questions?"

"No sir," replied both men.

"Good," Fletcher said, reached for the IMC and piped. "Set General Quarters, Intercept. Set General Quarters, Intercept. This is not a Drill."

Once the necessary information was exchanged, Fletcher announced, "Take the Conn for a minute, Chief. I'll be right back."

Fletcher went to his stateroom, unlocked the safe, and took out a canvas-wrapped bundle. "Here we go again," he thought, buckling on the web belt it contained.

By the time he got back, *Gallops Island* was on a course to intercept the go-fast, angling to come in from the north. The waiting began as the helo moved in from the south.

US Coast Guard Cutter *Bibb*

While she had been talking with *Gallops Island*, the three people Tipper asked for had gathered around the chart table.

"General Quarters is set and the Flight Deck is manned and ready," Lieutenant Commander Dick Samualson, the executive officer, reported.

Operations officer Lieutenant Sally Amooro was next. "Weapons manned and ready. The over the horizon boat is ready with the crew standing by."

"The helicopter is manned and ready with the weapon mounted, but not loaded," said Lieutenant Amy Forrest, the helo pilot, finishing the reports.

Tipper nodded. "Very well. We'll follow standard procedures during this evolution," she continued. "Forrest, the helo will force the go-fast toward *Gallops Island* for interception and boarding, or, if necessary, you'll disable the go-fast with fire from your .50 caliber rifle. We'll keep *Bibb's* OTH in reserve until the go-fast is stopped. Any questions?"

There were none.

"Keep in mind the possibility that the go-fast may not stop when approached as they have in the past, and may actually fire on any approaching ship, aircraft or Boarding Detachment," she said, echoing Fletcher's comment to his officers.

"So," Tipper looked at the group around her on the Bridge, "caution your crews again to be extra careful. Forrest, I know it'll be uncomfortable, but I want you and your crew to wear body armor."

"Aye, aye, Captain," said a surprised Forrest.

Tipper nodded again. "That's all. Dismissed."

When Forrest got to the helicopter she asked Gunners Mate Second Class Larry Katula to get the body armor for them.

"What are the flak jackets for?" asked her co-pilot, Ensign Paul Grabowski. "We're airdales, not Boarding Detachments."

"Captain's orders. There's a chance the bad guys may shoot back, or shoot first," said Forrest. "Getting shot could put a crimp in your career."

The gunner returned in time to hear the last remark. Without a word, he handed each officer two sets of armor.

Furrowing his brow, Grabowski said, "We can only wear one at a time. Why the spare set?"

"These things only work if you're hit in either the front or back, not while sitting down. So, put the second one under you. That way you protect not only your career but also any future generations of Grabowskis you have planned," answered Katula with a smile.

"Good thought, thanks." Forrest grinned. "Now let's get this show on the road."

US Coast Guard Helicopter

After clearing *Bibb's* Flight Deck, the helo quickly overtook the fleeing go-fast.

As the target came into sight, Katula's voice came over the intercom. "We got a problem, folks."

Forrest looked up from the instruments and keyed her mike, "Homeplate, Third base, this is Shortstop. There are two fastballs, not one. Repeat, there are two fastballs. They're splitting up. One is continuing east and the other is peeling off towards Third base." From her altitude, she could see *Gallops Island*, but was sure the go-fasts couldn't.

Tipper was in the *Bibb's* Combat Information Center when Forrest's message came in. "You have them on the scope?" she asked the radar operator.

"Yes, Captain. Second contact designated Bravo."

"What's Bravo's track look like?"

"I concur with Shortstop. It's headed for Third base."

"Good," she replied, picking up the mike. "Third base, Shortstop, this is Homeplate. Here's how we'll do this. Shortstop, you close on the one in front of you. You'll have to stop him on your own. Third base, the second one's yours. From our plot, it looks like he's got nowhere to run."

"Shortstop, roger," acknowledged Forrest.

"Third base, roger," echoed Fletcher.

"Homeplate, we are commencing our run," finished Forrest, turning towards the target.

With Forrest flying the aircraft, Grabowski watched the go-fast. He saw one of the men in the boat stand up and point something at them.

"Oh my God, he's got a gun! Bank right, bank right!" he yelled as the windshield cracked, pieces of the instrument panel blew upward and a line of holes marched across the cockpit. He was whacked back in the seat as Forrest pulled hard right, almost putting the helo on its side. Katula was flung hard against his harness as the helo turned, a burst of fire puncturing the skin of the helo where he'd been standing.

Adrenalin poured through Forrest as she hauled her wounded aircraft out of range.

"Anyone hit?" she asked as she scanned the instruments to see if anything vital had been damaged. Amazingly, they were still flying.

"Homeplate, Third base, we're hit. The bastard shot at us," she reported, sounding calm, belying the fact she was soaked in sweat and shaking. "No casualties and no major damage to the aircraft."

That last statement wasn't completely true: The windshield was shattered, part of the control panel had been shot to hell, and the pilot was shaken up.

"Shortstop, this is Homeplate," Tipper's voice crackled in her ears. "Return to base, we'll do this another way."

"Will you be able to get to these guys with the OTH?" Forrest asked.

"Negative. We're too far and the target has turned toward Cuban waters," answered Tipper.

"You two willing to make another run?" Forrest asked her crew over the intercom. "Katula, you first."

Katula replied, "If we shoot first this time, let's do it."

"I'd hate to let the SOBs go," said Grabowski. "I don't want to tempt fate, but I'm beside you all the way."

"Homeplate, we're going back. This time we'll be ready," Forrest said as she banked the helo around.

"Negative, repeat negative. Return to the ship." Tipper's voice was even firmer than usual.

Forrest ignored the order as she concentrated on her attack, dropping down until the helo's skids were almost touching the waves. "Okay, I'm going to come in on his stern. Katula, give a shout when we're close enough to shoot into his engines. Once he's hit, we'll slow down and stay back out of range until *Bibb* arrives. Any questions?"

"Just one. What will we do when he fires back?" asked Katula.

"Shoot him."

"Amy, we can't do that," protested Grabowski. "The rules of engagement say we need authorization before opening fire, and then only to disable the boat."

Forrest shook her head. "I'd rather be alive for my court-martial than the guest of honor at a burial at sea. If we wait for Captain Tipper to check with HQ this guy will be long gone."

Grabowski didn't say anything else; he was watching the go-fast getting closer.

US Coast Guard Cutter *Gallops Island*

Debricko and Ashton were standing behind Fletcher when the report came from the *Bibb* that there were two boats.

Debricko asked, "Are we going to change the operation? I recommend that we get the second team set and the boat ready to assist Shortstop. That'll save some time."

"I agree. Chief, will you take care of it?" Fletcher replied.

"Aye, aye, sir," said Ashton and headed below.

The radio snapped to life. "Homeplate, Third base, we're hit, the bastard shot at us. No casualties and no major damage to the aircraft."

"She's got guts to take incoming and stay cool," Fletcher said, listening until the rest of the exchange between Tipper and Forrest ended with: "Homeplate, we're going back. This time we'll be ready."

"She's out of her fucking mind!" exploded Fletcher, rattling Debricko and the Lookout. He assessed the new situation in a split second. "Alright—Ed, we may have to use the second boat to recover what's left of the helo's crew. Also, when we get in range of our target, give them one chance to stop, then fire across their bow. Make sure the crew knows what happened to the helo when they tried to do it by the rules. I don't what anyone shot."

"Aye, aye, sir." With that, Debricko left the Flying Bridge.

US Coast Guard Cutter Helicopter

She could almost feel the wave tops as the helo skimmed toward the outlaw boat. By coming up directly behind it, they offered a difficult target.

"OK, Skipper, we're there," said Katula.

Forrest flared slightly to the right and the gunner opened fire, walking the bullets over the water and into the go-fast's engines. Just as Katula pulled the trigger, the go-fast's gunner stood up, bringing a weapon to his shoulder. Without hesitation, Katula continued swinging the bucking fifty-caliber rifle forward.

Forrest saw it all from the cockpit. As the outlaw gunner popped up, she thought, "We're dead."

But Katula's shots hit him and he was thrown over the side. The go-fast's engines were smoking as it slewed to a stop, dead in the water, the second man raising his hands, out of the fight.

"Nice shooting," Forrest said to her gunner, glancing at Grabowski next to her. "You okay, Paul?" she asked, noticing he was shaking, his face drawn. A nod was his only reply.

"Homeplate, Third base, this is Shortstop. We got him, he's dead in the water," radioed Forrest, omitting the fact that one man had been killed in the attack.

"Good work," responded Tipper, deciding now was not the time to handle Forrest's insubordination. "We're launching the OTH. Can you stay there until it arrives?"

"Roger, we'll be here," answered Forrest.

US Coast Guard Cutter *Gallops Island*

"One down, one to go," said Fletcher. Picking up the ship's intercom, he relayed the news of Shortstop's success to his crew. "Now it's our turn." The second go-fast was in sight but apparently hadn't yet seen *Gallops Island*.

"Ed, we're going to handle this differently from what was originally planned," Mark said. "When the boat gets in range, we'll open fire across his bow; that way there will be no question of our intentions. Also, I'll lead the Boarding Team."

"That's my job, Captain. Don't you trust me?" Debricko protested.

"I trust you with my life, but we've never seen two go-fasts together and they've never tried to shoot down a helo," replied Fletcher. "That's why I'm going over."

When the go-fast saw them, Fletcher's gunners opened fire without warning. With bullets ripping the water in front of it, the go-fast tried to escape, but it was trapped. Its engines stopped and it lay in the swells, waiting to be boarded.

"That was too easy. This smells," thought Fletcher as the Boarding Team approached. When they came alongside, Fletcher heard the go-fast's engines rumbling at idle and saw the two-man crew standing by the controls. One man had his hands raised while the other had one hand raised and was scratching his crotch with the other.

Fletcher went aboard first, the rest of the team spreading to his right and left as they followed. The second team member started to move toward the crew when the first smuggler spun around and shoved the idling engines in gear. Thrown backward when the boat took off, Fletcher watched the second smuggler pull a pistol out of his pants and open fire.

GM3 Carol Duane screamed as a bullet tore into her leg. Fletcher looked over to see blood seeping from her thigh. The other team member lay unconscious against the sacks of cargo.

Fletcher ducked as bullets whipped around him. There was nowhere to go. The go-fast was keeping the boarding team's boat between it and *Gallops Island* so the cutter couldn't fire.

The shooting had stopped. Pulling his pistol, Fletcher eased around the left corner of the sacks and stood up, facing the control station.

There was only one man there, his back towards Fletcher. Shifting his sights a little to the right, Fletcher fired twice, hitting the smuggler in the shoulder, knocking him into the console.

Something struck Fletcher's ribs, pitching him hard against the side of the boat. Swinging around, Fletcher let go three fast shots and scuttled forward. Two more shots hit the bags by his head. Fletcher moved further right, stood up, and fired twice at his briefly-glimpsed attacker.

As he was reaching for a fresh magazine, Fletcher looked up to see the second smuggler standing on top of the cargo looking down at him.

"You should be more careful with that antique pistol of yours." The man pointed his own weapon at Fletcher's face. "Only seven shots. Too bad. Perhaps you'll remember that for the next time. But, of course, for you, there won't be a next time," he smirked, savoring the moment.

Centering his antique on the smuggler's forehead, Mark said, "I have eight rounds, not seven. You remember that for the next time." He pulled the trigger. "But, of course, for you, there won't be a next time."

PART III
DAYS

08

SUNDAY

**Private Aviation Terminal,
Baltimore Washington International Airport, 1:30 PM Eastern Time**

This was the first weekend Ann Gallaher had had off in months, and she'd flown to Saint Michael's on Maryland's beautiful eastern shore. The trip had been a dual celebration: Friday her divorce was finalized and Saturday she turned fifty. The best part of the trip was the chance to fly again, one of two things in her life she took pleasure in doing. The other was her job as

Vice Commandant of the Coast Guard. Just running the post-flight inspection on the rented Beechcraft Bonanza brought a sense of contentment.

Just as she finished the inspection, her cell phone rang. "What now?" she thought.

The number showing on Caller ID brought her up short; it was her boss, Admiral Vincent Story, Commandant of the Coast Guard.

"Good afternoon, Admiral," Ann answered.

"Hello, Ann. There's an emergency. Are you still in the air?"

"No, Admiral, I'm on the ground. What's going on?"

"There have been two simultaneous terrorist attacks: one on a Navy cruiser in Norfolk and the other on a cruise ship in Seattle. We have few details yet, except that there are a lot of casualties on both ships. Ann, how fast can you get to the White House?"

Shaken, Ann replied: "Ninety minutes to go home, change into uniform and get into DC."

"Skip the uniform."

"Aye, aye, Admiral. I'll be there in less than an hour."

"Good. See you there."

Closing her phone, Ann took her bag out of the plane and headed to the terminal, her mind outlining the basics of what would need to be done, with the specifics to be filled in later. Reaching her car, she whispered a prayer for the victims.

The Whitehouse, Washington, D.C., 2:30 PM, Eastern Time

Taking her seat in the underground Briefing Room, Ann saw that everyone was wearing casual clothes, an indication of the seriousness of the situation. Worrying about pressed uniforms at a time like this was just Mickey Mouse nonsense.

"Attention," was called as President John Woodbird entered.

"Please be seated and let's get started," he said. "We'll start with the cruiser. Larry, what do you have?" The question was directed at General Lawrence Oakly, Chairman of the Joint Chiefs of Staff.

"Mr. President, I'm going to cut out the middle man and let Admiral Nathan answer that," said Oakly, deferring to Admiral George Nathan, Chief of Naval Operations, the man in charge of the Navy.

Nathan began, "I'll start by showing you footage of the attack made by a local news station helicopter."

It was like watching a Greek tragedy; each person knew what the end would be. They saw the *Concord*'s crew on the deck before the camera shifted to the security boats as they raced to intercept the intruders.

"Oh my God," Ann heard an unidentified voice whisper as the guns opened fire, "it was a perfect setup."

It wasn't a long film, but the horror of it hit each of them hard.

When it ended, Nathan continued: "*Concord* has a 550 person crew; of those, 210 were killed and 125 injured or wounded. I'm sure the casualty figure will go up. At present, thirty-seven are unaccounted for.

"As you saw, the cruiser's bow is aground on the left side of the channel, while her stern is resting on the bottom on the right side of the channel. As of now, Norfolk, Hampton Roads and Newport News are closed to all shipping. It will be several hours, at least, before we'll know for how long."

This grim news was met by silence. There were no questions; each person understood the implications of having three major port areas, including a major naval base, sealed off.

"Thank you Admiral," said the President. "Let's proceed to the cruise ship. Vince, what do you have?"

"Unfortunately, very little," Story began. He briefly outlined the attack and ramming, concluding: "The force of the blow, combined with the outgoing tidal current, swung the ship broadside in the channel. As of twenty minutes ago, both vessels were reported in the middle of the channel, on fire and listing heavily. There's a strong possibility that they'll both capsize, closing off Seattle and Tacoma. Our efforts are directed at rescuing the passengers and crew.

Story looked around at the group of intent faces. "And one more thing: There's an unconfirmed report that just before she rammed the *Polaris Queen,* six men from the fishing vessel escaped in a small boat."

For just a moment the President lowered his head, but then he sat up and squared his shoulders. "Recommendations?"

Vice President Oliver Stanfield spoke up. "Although there were military and civilian targets, I feel that there should be a coordinated response, with Homeland Security in charge. We'll activate the National Incident Management System and, under it, the Incident Command System."

[NOTE: The National Incident Management System (NIMS) was established on March 1, 2004 by Homeland Security Presidential Directive (HSPD)-5 to manage Domestic Incidents. Directive addresses
- Incident Command System
- Preparedness
- Communications and Information Systems
- Joint Information System (JIS)
- NIMS Integration Center (NIC)

NIMS provides a consistent nationwide template to enable all government, private-sector, and nongovernmental organizations to work together during domestic incidents.]

"I agree," said Nathan, "as long as the Coast Guard takes the lead. Two attacks, two major ports' facilities closed, this is their bailiwick."

There was a murmur of consent around the table. Story gave Gallaher a small shrug as if to say: "I told you we'd get it." Ann acknowledged the gesture with a nod.

The President turned to Steven Highland, Secretary of Homeland Security. "Steve, what are your thoughts?"

Highland had been both looking forward to and dreading the question. He wanted to head the operation; the political rewards and media recognition would make him a national figure. There was going to be a lot of fallout from the attacks and he wanted to be seen as the leader who brought the terrorists to justice.

To complicate matters, he didn't like either Story or Gallaher. Highland was sure Gallaher would be put in charge, and that rankled. He had fought against her promotion to Vice Commandant, even though it lost him political support from women's groups. He knew more about fund raising and political maneuvering than he did about maritime security operations, but this was too good an opportunity to miss.

"Mr. President, as Secretary of Homeland Security, I should head the team."

"I disagree," said Bob Lopez, the FBI Director. "You don't have the experience necessary to coordinate the efforts."

Immediately the Secretary of Defense said: "I concur with Bob. The Coast Guard has the experts in this area, and most of the resources will come from them anyway."

Instead of directly addressing the issue, the President asked: "Vince, who will you put in charge?"

Story answered without hesitation. "Admiral Gallaher."

"Good choice, Vince," said Oakly, which earned him a venomous look from Highland.

Nathan caught the look, and, knowing Highland's dislikes, added, "It makes sense having Admiral Gallaher run the show. She's experienced as well as senior enough to get things done."

"Alright," said the President, "Admiral Gallaher, you'll be in charge. What's your first step?"

Taking a breath, Ann addressed the group: "First, we order all Coast Guard units on alert and beef-up port security patrols. We can't shut every port, but we can work to prevent further attacks.

"The next step will be to set up the Incident Command

System here, with subordinate ICSs at Coast Guard Atlanta and Pacific Area headquarters, and in all ports as deemed necessary. As you all know, this allows us to tap resources at the federal, state and local levels. I should be able to pull it together within the next four to six hours.

[NOTE: The Incident Command System.(ICS) is a management system designed to enable effective and efficient domestic incident management by integrating a combination of facilities, equipment, personnel, procedures, and communications operating within a common organizational structure, designed to enable effective and efficient domestic incident management. A basic premise of ICS is that it is widely applicable. It is used to organize both near-term and long-term field-level operations for a broad spectrum of emergencies, from small to complex incidents, both natural and manmade. ICS is used by all levels of government—federal, state, local, and tribal—as well as by many in the private-sector and nongovernmental organizations. ICS is also applicable across disciplines. It is normally structured to facilitate activities in five major functional areas: Command, Operations, Planning, Logistics, and Finance and Administration.]

"General Oakly, will you detail a liaison from the Joint Chiefs to me, with authority to act in your name?"

"Of course, I'll have someone for you within the hour."

Ann kept moving. "Director Lopez and Director Trilby, may I have someone from the FBI and CIA?" Both men readily agreed to the request.

"Mr. President, obviously the rescue, salvage and pollution-control parts of the operation will be well-covered by the press.

However, even though the ICS has an Information Officer, it would be best if what we're doing is kept as quiet as possible."

"Admiral Gallaher, the White House will try to keep the media off your back," the President assured her. Then he asked the group, "Is there anything else at present?"

Getting negative responses from everyone, he said, "We'll reconvene in four hours. Please keep me advised of all developments. The media will have a field day with this, and I expect there'll be Congressional investigations, however ill-founded."

With that, the meeting ended. Just as the President was heading for the door, an aide entered and handed him a package.

"This is for Admiral Story," the aide said. "It was delivered to Coast Guard headquarters twenty minutes ago, and after seeing the first few minutes, they sent it over. Apparently it's from the terrorists."

The DVD was set up and lights were dimmed as the group settled back into their seats.

Seiako International, New York City, 3:00 PM, Eastern Time

The bank of flat-panel television screens covering one office wall showed a kaleidoscope of horrific images interspersed with somber talking heads, pontificating about the meaning of those images. A ringing cell phone broke the stillness.

Evelyn LaBlanc answered it with the usual single word: "Yes?"

"You've seen the reports?"

"I'm watching them now."

"So we're on our way."

"I am well pleased. Is our friend set for part two?"

"In two days. That should give them time to grasp the significance of what's going on."

"Good. I'll be meeting with our other friend this evening," replied LaBlanc, breaking the connection.

Pushing a button on the desk phone, she asked: "Is the jet ready, Gwen?"

"Yes."

"Have the car brought around, we'll leave now."

. LaBlanc gathered her thoughts as the limo sped toward Teterboro Airport. All had proceeded as planned, and that boded well for the rest of the operation. Ryse/al-Hishma was the perfect foil. His attacks would focus attention elsewhere while the real threat went unnoticed.

Tonight's dinner in DC would be very informative, although the man she was meeting was a venal fool.

09

Coast Guard Headquarters, Washington, D.C., 4:00 PM, Eastern Time

Located at 2100 Second Street SW, the outside of Coast Guard headquarters looks like a second-rate office building rented out to third-rate companies. It sits in a neighborhood filled with low-income housing, auto-repair shops, and dingy diners connected by pothole-laced streets. Behind the building is the Anacostia River. Two small marinas flank the lower right and left corners at forty-five degree angles. The building's reception and security area matches the exterior impression of a low-rent operation, with worn tile on the floor and battered walls painted a military-industrial shade of beige. The fluorescently lit hallways are depressingly similar in appearance and the décor isn't up to the standards of a moderately successful financial institution.

However, its singularly unimpressive appearance belies the fact the US Coast Guard is a unique and powerful organization. The United States Coast Guard is the oldest continuous sea-going service of this nation.

Founded in 1790 by Alexander Hamilton, the first Secretary of the Treasury, as the Revenue Cutter Service, it was originally composed of ten schooners used for the collection of custom duties and the enforcement of the revenue laws. The Coast Guard came into being in 1915 when Congress passed and President Wilson signed "An Act to create the Coast Guard…which shall constitute part of the military forces of the United States."

It was formed by combining the Revenue Marine and the Life Saving Service. Between 1919 and 1942, the Federal Lighthouse Service, Steamboat Inspection Service and the Bureau of Navigation were amalgamated into the Coast Guard, thus creating its present form.

It is now a military, multi-mission, maritime service within the Department of Homeland Security, and one of the nation's five armed services. Its core roles are to protect the public, the environment, and U.S. economic and security interests in any maritime region in which those interests may be at risk, including international waters and America's coasts, ports, and inland waterways.

Under Title 14 U. S. Code, Chapter 5, Sections 89 and 143 (14 USC § 98 and §143) Coast Guard personal E-4 (i.e. Petty Officer Third Class) and above are Federal Law Enforcement and Customs officers. This entails the following:

1) carry a firearm;
2) execute and serve any order, warrant, subpoena, summons, or other process issued under the authority of the United States; and
3) make an arrest without a warrant for any offense against the United States committed in the officer's presence or for a felony, cognizable under the laws of the United States committed outside the officer's presence if the officer has reasonable grounds to believe that the person to be arrested has committed or is committing a felony.

No other government department, including the FBI, Secret Service, Customs, DEA, and ATF, have as broad a range of powers as does the Coast Guard.

In contrast to the exterior shabbiness, the Commandant's office was comfortably furnished. One wall was covered in baseball caps from different units; family photos took up another. Leather chairs and a small couch surrounding a coffee table occupied one corner. Late afternoon filtered through louvered blinds, giving the room a gentle feel, a sharp contrast to its tense occupants.

Sitting in one of the chairs, Ann took a sip of her coffee and muttered to Story, "I need this coffee like I need another hole in my head."

They had just finished conference calls with the Coast Guard Atlantic and Pacific Area commanders, discussing the manning of their respective Incident Command System as well as additional security arrangements. Following the calls they reviewed the terrorist-produced tape and formulated responses to the demands it contained.

"Agreeing to an immediate withdrawal of our forces from Iraq and paying the terrorists one billion dollars are not going to happen," said Story. "We need to beef up port security and try to determine the most likely targets. The working assumption is that there will be more attacks."

"Also, what's the connection to Mark Fletcher and why will the terrorist only deal with him?"

The last demand was that Lieutenant Mark Fletcher, US Coast Guard, be the contact for all future communications.

"The Court of Inquiry hasn't completed its investigation of the shooting Fletcher was involved in yesterday, but there's nothing so far that links him to any terrorists. He did serve in the Persian Gulf War, but never came into contact with the Iraqis," Ann answered. "With everything going on I didn't tell you earlier, but before leaving the White House, I had our Duty Officer order Fletcher picked up from *Gallops Island* and brought here ASAP. He'll be arriving in about five minutes."

That time was spent discussing what assets would be needed and which people were to be assigned the key positions in the Headquarters Incident Command System structure. This information would be presented at the next White House briefing. Another crucial item was salvaging the *Polaris Queen*. Ann called Todd Busch at TITAN Salvage to arrange a contract. Having worked with the Coast Guard before, Todd agreed to have a team in Seattle by Monday morning to begin surveying the wreck.

A sharp, double rap on the door made them both look up. Story said, "Come."

Opening the door, Mark Fletcher marched in, stopping three feet in front of the Commandant's desk, and standing at attention, his eyes fixed on the wall behind the seated admiral. "Lieutenant Fletcher, reporting as ordered."

Sitting at a table to one side, Ann looked Fletcher over carefully. Dressed in jeans and a short-sleeved shirt, he didn't seem at all flustered by his unexplained orders to report to the Commandant. She wasn't sure whether that was a good or bad reaction, but would reserve judgment

"At ease, Lieutenant," said Story. "I'm sorry we're meeting at such a difficult time. I met your father years ago when I was an ensign. He's a fine man."

"Thank you, Admiral," said Mark, relaxing slightly.

"Have you met Admiral Gallaher?"

Ann came over and introduced herself. Mark had only seen Admiral Gallaher's official photograph. Shaking her hand, he thought her official photo was unflattering; it didn't convey the intelligence in her eyes or how good-looking she really was.

Once they were seated at the conference table, Story began. "Fletcher, the terrorist claiming responsibility for today's attacks sent a tape with his demands. The last demand was that you be the sole contact person."

Fletcher stared at the Commandant for a moment. "Why me?"

"That's what we'd like to know. Starting with the recent shooting in the Florida Straits, is there any time you might have crossed paths with these people?" asked Ann.

"I can't think of anything off hand," replied Mark, getting up and helping himself to a cup of coffee, after first offering it to the admirals. Returning to his chair, he was about halfway through the cup when Ann saw him stiffen.

"What is it?"

"There is something that only seven people know about. In the Persian Gulf, I went on a mission with five SEALs. I shot one of the attackers as we extracted from the beach."

Story said, "There's nothing in your service record about the shooting."

"The SEAL team CO said not to mention anything about it. None of the team was killed, so it was easy to cover."

"Were you out of your mind?" asked Ann sharply. "What possessed you to do it?"

"One of the team broke his ankle during an operation, and they needed someone to drive the boat. My CO on *Evans* wasn't aware of the mission, and neither was I until arriving at SEAL headquarters. It sounded like a good idea at the time," Mark answered with a shrug.

Ann was not amused by Fletcher's apparent unconcern about the consequences of his actions. "So part of this trouble can be attributed to your irresponsibility in not reporting this to your superiors?"

The hostility in Gallaher's voice caught Mark off guard.

"With all due respect, Admiral, the mission was classified at the time, and no one outside the SEAL team was authorized access to the information. Therefore, I didn't submit a report to my CO."

Story said: "Fletcher, write down the team number and the member's names. Maybe one of them will remember something."

Mark complied with the request and handed the list to him.

"Go watch the DVD," said Ann. "You may recognize the terrorist. Then we have to be at the next White House briefing in an hour. And that 'we' includes you, Fletcher."

10

Coast Guard Headquarters, Washington, D.C., 8:00 PM, Eastern Time

"It's been a long day, so we'll keep this as brief as possible," Ann said to four key members of the Incident Command System staff.

"Since this is our first meeting, I'll start by introducing the Command Staff Officers. Admiral Ken James, CO of the Deployable Operations Group; Captain Doug Briggs, Operations Section; and Ms. Robin Candler from Homeland Security will handle Intelligence. Logistics will be the purview of Commander Julia Kidd; and, finally, Finance and Administration will be under Lieutenant Commander Jonathan Romanski. Be nice to Jon because if you need money, he's the man."

This brought a ripple of polite laughter from the group, slightly easing the tension.

"I know it's short notice, but by nine o'clock Monday morning, I want each of you to have selected your subordinate group members and specialists. All of you have seen the DVD from the terrorist. As you know, the deadline for meeting his demands has been set at 10:00 AM Eastern time, Tuesday morning.

"The President has said we won't pay the one billion dollars demanded. This gives us just under thirty-two hours in which to work."

Pausing, Ann turned and gestured for the man sitting behind her to stand. "This is Lieutenant Mark Fletcher. As you know, he's the only person the terrorist will talk to. We're trying to discovery the reason behind this seemingly inconsistent demand, but, so far, there aren't any answers.

"Do any of you have questions about the assignments before we break up?"

Robin said, "I'll need someone from Coast Guard Intelligence. Do you know who might be available?"

Before Ann could reply, Mark bent down and whispered a name to her. She shot a questioning look at him, and he said: "Her last assignment was with Atlantic Area Intelligence and she's available."

Ann mentally ran though the pros and cons of his suggestion, and then nodded her agreement. Turning back to Robin, she said, "I'll assign Lieutenant Amy Forrest to work with you. I'll have Fletcher bring her to your office in the morning."

"Thanks, I look forward to meeting her," replied Robin. She realized Gallaher didn't know she knew about Forrest's violent part in that drug bust. She'd wait to meet and talk with Forrest before coming to any conclusions about her.

There were no other questions, so Ann concluded the meeting. "I've given you a lot to do and not much time to do it. I'll see you again at nine."

La Petit Femme Bistro, Georgetown, 9:00 PM, Eastern Time

A single candle radiated its soft glow in the curtained dining alcove, engendering a sense of tranquility. The mood was broken when the man began whining about his day.

"Ann Gallaher will be heading the ICS, a job that should have been mine," moaned Highland, beginning to feel angry all over again. "It's a once-in-a-lifetime opportunity to gain national recognition."

"I agree that you're the one to do the job," said LaBlanc. "Perhaps I can help you. With my position in the international shipping industry, I have an interest in thwarting further attacks. As a consultant to your department, it's reasonable that you'd call on my expertise to assist in this crisis." She took a sip of her brandy. "Why don't you suggest that to the President? I'm sure he'll accept the idea, if for no other reason than to placate you. Once I'm in place, I will have opportunities to strengthen your position."

Highland smiled. "That's a very good idea, Evelyn. And the sooner you're in place the better. You're a good friend." Highland stood, reenergized by this new idea. "I've got to get back and see what the latest developments are. I'll call you as soon as I speak to the President and Admiral Story about your offer."

Finishing the last of the brandy, LaBlanc smiling, thinking her manipulation had worked very well. Highland's vanity and lust for power made him almost as good a foil as Ryse. Glancing at the table, she wasn't surprised Highland had left the check for her to pay.

It was a small price to pay compared to the millions of dollars she had invested to further his political career. Now those millions would be returned tenfold. And she had an added safeguard Highland was not aware of, a part of the package Demivov brought to her through their business arrangement.

Highland, as an under secretary of state on a fact-finding mission to Kosovo, had been filmed performing some very unusual sexual acts with a thirteen-year-old prostitute. When confronted with the tapes and a demand for money by Demivov, he countered by demanding a copy of the tape for his personal library and a partnership in the operation. Upon returning to Washington, he had discretely provided selected individuals with whatever met his or her sexual needs. This, coupled with a seemingly endless supply of funds, assured Highland's rapid political rise.

Now it was payback time.

Georgetown, District of Columbia, 10:30 PM, Eastern Time

Robin Candler and Doug Briggs arrived home at the same time. As the door closed, they hugged tightly. When they separated, Robin collapsed on the couch while Doug went to the kitchen and poured two glasses of wine. After handing Robin a glass, Doug settled down next to her. He asked his lover and soul mate, "You okay?"

"Oh, Doug, what a mess," she said. "All those people dead or injured and two ships sunk. How do we deal with this?"

"The best way we can. That's a trite answer, but that's it. Ann's good and she's picked good people to work with, present company included," Doug replied, toasting her with his glass.

Robin smiled. "At least we'll be keeping the same hours for a change, a straight-out twenty-four per day. I'm not sure if I was more surprised when the admiral assigned Forrest to my team or that she did it on a suggestion from Fletcher."

"That surprised me too, so I checked with a friend who worked with Forrest at Atlantic Area. He says she's sharp and did a terrific job. I don't believe Gallaher just dumped her on you out of convenience."

"What do you know about Fletcher?"

"Another good question. He's quite a character from what I hear. Rumor has it that one of his forefathers was a smuggler who changed his ways and helped set up the Revenue Marine Service, the forerunner of the Coast Guard, in the late 1700s. Mark seems to be a throwback who would be as comfortable climbing the rigging of a sailing ship as he is captaining a diesel-powered cutter."

Robin laughed. "That last part sounds like you."

"That was part of my misspent youth, long before I met you," Doug countered with a smile. "And, from what I've heard, you were involved in some pretty hairy operations with the FBI counter-terrorist group before your transfer to Homeland Security a couple of years ago."

Robin sighed. "Please, I'm still having nightmares about those days."

Reaching over, Doug gathered her in his arms. "I know. Let's go to bed. It's going to be a long day."

11

MONDAY

Coast Guard Headquarters, Washington, D.C., 8:00AM, Eastern Time

Ann was enjoying her first cup of coffee when the phone rang. "This is Admiral Gallaher."

"Good morning, Ann. It's Vince."

"Good morning, Admiral. What may I do for you?"

"I just had a call from the President. He says Highland feels that the ICS team should include an advisor from the international maritime industry."

Ann paused a moment, thinking. "I don't agree with that suggestion for several reasons. You know our first priority is security. The deployment of forces, access to both domestic and international intelligence, and the Command, Communications and Control aspects of the operations are all on a need-to-know basis. Any outsider is a security risk."

"I understand, and I voiced those points to the President, but Highland has a lot of political influence. Also, Highland's ego took a beating by not being put in charge of the ICS, so we need do some damage control," explained Story.

"Does the secretary have someone specific in mind?" asked Ann, trying to remain calm.

Story took a deep breath. "He said that an international maritime consultant named Evelyn LaBlanc has offered her services."

"Did Highland say when this offer was made?"

"According to the President, it was last night. Apparently Highland and Ms. LaBlanc meet for dinner once a month, and last night was the night."

Ann raised an eyebrow. "What a coincidence."

"Yes, I thought so too," replied Story. "You might want to keep that in mind when dealing with her."

Reluctantly accepting the inevitable, Ann said, "Thanks for the advice, and I definitely will. The ICS meets again in an hour. When will our new member be joining us?"

"She'll be at your office in thirty minutes. I thought you two should meet as soon as possible to discuss the situation and her role."

"Thank you, Admiral. It should be an interesting meeting."

"Ann, I'm not any happier about this than you are, but Highland sandbagged us on this one."

Coast Guard Headquarters, Washington, D.C., 8:00AM, Eastern Time

"Come in," said Robin to the knock on her office door. Looking up, she saw Lieutenants Forrest and Fletcher standing in her office doorway.

Her first thought was that, from what she knew, they couldn't be more different in appearance and more alike in temperament. Fletcher was tanned, six feet tall and of medium build, with eyes the same color brown as his hair. The petite, ebony-skinned Forrest, her lustrous black hair pulled into a bun, returned Robin's scrutiny through intelligent green eyes.

"Hi, I'm Robin Candler." She extended her hand, first to Amy, then Mark. "Please sit down. Forrest, I know we're short on time, and there are two things I need you to start on immediately."

Amy nodded, ready to go.

"First, after the attack on the cruise ship in Seattle, there was an unconfirmed report that the terrorists escaped in a small boat. Track down the survivor who made that report and see if he or she is in shape to be flown here as soon as possible."

"Aye, aye, ma'am," Amy answered promptly.

Before giving Amy the second task, Robin addressed Mark. "Fletcher, Admiral Gallaher gave me the details of your heretofore unreported Iraqi operation."

Amy's head snapped toward Fletcher. "His what?"

Robin filled her in: "While stationed in the Persian Gulf in 2003, he agreed to help land a SEAL team behind the lines in Iraq. The team was ambushed and fought its way out. Just as they were clearing the beach, Fletcher shot one of the attackers."

Amy looked at Mark. "Were you out of your cotton-pickin' mind?"

Mark shrugged. "It was supposed to be a beach party. I shouldn't have trusted those SEALs."

The two women just looked at him, then at each other, shaking their heads in resignation.

Taking control of the conversation again and handing Amy a piece of paper, Robin said: "Here are the names of the team members Fletcher gave to Admiral Gallaher. One of them may be able to help us identify the terrorist on the tape. See if the Navy can track them down immediately if not sooner."

"No one at the Pentagon is going to respond quickly to a request from a mere lieutenant," countered Amy.

"Admiral Gallaher told me that might be a problem, so you have authorization to call Admiral Nathan, Chief of Naval Operations, to get what you need. That's his private number at the bottom of the list," Robin said. "Okay, that's it for now. Forrest, your office is two doors down the hall. Fletcher, go with her and help coordinate the effort to track down the SEAL team."

Coast Guard Headquarters, Washington, D.C., 8:30AM, Eastern Time

Evelyn LaBlanc arrived at Ann's office on time. After exchanging introductions, LaBlanc's assistant, Gwen Golden, was asked to wait in the outer office. Ann and Evelyn settled around a small conference table with two cups of fresh coffee.

Ann addressed the slim, elegantly dressed woman seated across from her. "Ms. LaBlanc, I appreciate your offer to assist us in this crisis, but it would be precedent-setting for someone in your position to be allowed full access to the ICS."

"Admiral Gallaher, I understand your position and the sensitivity of the situation. However, I have extensive experience in international maritime operations, and a vested interest is seeing that nothing interferes with my business," replied LaBlanc with a small accommodating smile. "To that end, I can offer you immediate access to worldwide shipping information as well as my own, highly developed intelligence system."

Ann replied, "That is a generous offer, but, as I'm sure you know, we have our own extensive resources in those areas."

"I know what resources you have, and, unlike yours, my own extend into the Chinese and North Korean intelligence networks, among others."

Ann sat back to consider the offer and the person who made it. She took a notable pause, controlling the conversation, but ignoring the warning sign flashing in her head, before she continued.

"I'm sure there are many things you know that I'm not aware of, and none of us ever stops learning. Since we'll be working together, please call me Ann."

Accepting her adversary's apparent surrender, LaBlanc replied: "Thank you, Ann, and please call me Evelyn."

12

Coast Guard Headquarters, Washington, D.C., 9:00AM, Eastern Time

When everyone was settled, Ann introduced Evelyn LaBlanc and explained her offer of assistance during the present crisis, ending with, "Ms. LaBlanc will liaise with your respective staffs because her information and resources are complementary to those in your areas."

With impressive aplomb, each of the ICS team concealed their surprise at this news.

Ann continued: "Moving forward, let's have the current status from each of you, starting with Intelligence."

Robin glanced briefly at her notes. "Preliminary information from the CIA, FBI, National Security Council and our overseas contacts points to a strictly maritime threat. Enhanced security at airports combined with the international effort to screen potential threats supports this conclusion.

"The demand made by the terrorist and the short space of time given to meet these demands leads us to believe that other attacks are planned."

"Ms. Candler, who, specifically, are your sources and what leads did you use to draw your conclusions?" asked LaBlanc.

Robin hid her annoyance at the interruption and answered, "It stands to reason that if the demands aren't met, there will be consequences. As for my sources, you aren't cleared for that information."

Without pause she went on. "Ports offer the largest number of potential targets that are difficult to defend. This fact has been mentioned in several speeches over the years and has been debated at length in Congress and in the press.

"From previous experience, we are assuming that all of the terrorist assault teams and their weapons are in place. INS and Customs are reviewing their records for the past six months to see if they can identify any visitors that came in and were lost in the crowd.

"While this is our operating principle, the President has ordered border security tightened and more visible security at airports. We can't take the chance that our assumptions are wrong," Robin concluded.

Ann spoke up. "Captain Briggs, please provide your initial analysis of the threat."

"Before providing specifics, I'll define the problem," Doug began. "There are 361 seaports in the United States, the majority of which are located along the East, Gulf and West Coasts. Of those ports, two-thirds of all ship-born trade is handled by only twelve of them. That doesn't sound like much of a security problem, but it is.

"A series of eight attacks can close all twelve ports, effectively stopping our economy.

They're choke points. While the attacks yesterday were tragic, they also closed three of the twelve harbors. That's twenty-five percent of our major ports, representing more than eighty billion dollars a year in cargo value. Also, by closing the ports, the terrorists can stop us from re-supplying our forces in Iraq."

Doug paused to take a drink of water. The others sat in stunned silence, the size of the figures and the simplicity of the concept was almost overwhelming.

More familiar with logistic operations than intelligence and security, Commander Kidd asked, "How tightly controlled is this information?"

Shaking his head slightly, Doug said: "It's not controlled at all. In fact, I got all this off the internet in less than half an hour. If I can do it, so can anyone else. As Ms. Candler said, our operating principle is that this will be a maritime threat aimed at the choke points."

"Do you think the terrorists will use weapons of mass destruction?" queried Jon Romanski.

"No," said Doug, without hesitation, "there's no need to. As we saw yesterday, conventional explosives and weapons were adequate. And, most importantly, they're easy to acquire and you don't need much training to use them. This type of threat was identified in the National Plan to Achieve Maritime Domain Awareness published in October 2005. I want to read you all a portion from the Strategic Environments Threats section:

> The vastness of the maritime domain provides great opportunities for exploitation by terrorists. The use of smaller commercial and recreational vessels closer to our shores and areas of interest to transport WMD/E is of significant concern. Additionally, terrorists can use large merchant ships to move powerful conventional explosives or WMD/E for detonation in a port or alongside an offshore facility. Terrorist groups have demonstrated a capacity to use shipping as a means of conveyance for positioning their agents, logistics support, and revenue generation. Terrorists have shown that they have the capability to use explosives-laden suicide boats as weapons. This capability could easily be used with merchant ships as kinetic weapons to ram another vessel, warship, port facility, or offshore platforms.

"As with the port information, this is available on the internet along with the entire structure of the ICS. The terrorists know how we operate, and we don't know a thing about them."

"How do we counter this?" asked LaBlanc.

"That's Admiral James's area, so I'll turn it over to him."

"Thanks, Captain," said Vice Admiral Ken James. "For the benefit of Ms. LaBlanc, I'll review the MDA zones and Expeditionary Harbor Defense package. The MDA begins with the Offshore Exclusive Economic Zone, extending from twelve to two hundred nautical miles. This is mainly patrolled by long-range aircraft. From the shore to twelve miles out is considered Territorial Sea which encompasses the Coastal Zone Interdiction Zone for our purposes. Third is the Inner Zone, including harbors and interstate navigable waterways.

"The Expeditionary Harbor Defense Package is a three-layer port defense system. This is employed within the US as well as overseas. Layer One deals with what we call C4ISR—which includes Command, Control, Communications, Computers, Intelligence, Surveillance and Reconnaissance—along with Interception, and Engagement. Part of the package are the Coast Guard VBSS—that's Visit, Board, Search and Seizure Teams. Layer Two is Coastal Interception and Engagement. And Layer Three is Harbor Defense. At present, our primary concern falls within Layer Three which is Harbor Defense."

When James finished, Jon Romanski asked: "And how much of this is classified information?"

"None of it. Like the info Doug presented, this, too, is on the internet," the admiral replied.

Ann asked: "What's the current status of the Deployable Operation Group's assets?"

"As you know the DOG has six component commands: the Maritime Security Response Team (MSRT); the Maritime Safety and Security Team (MSST); the Port Security Unit (PSU); the National Strike Force (NSF); the Naval Coastal Warfare Squadron (NCWS); and the Tactical Law Enforcement Team (TACLET).

"The twelve Marine Safety and Security Teams began operations Sunday evening. The Port Security Units are composed of Reservists and we're in the process of activating those units. They'll be operational by 2400 tonight.

"Our NCWS units, with their U.S. Navy personnel complements, will be ready by 2400 for deployment, as necessary, to augment the PSUs and MSSTs. The MSRT unit is standing by.

"Two National Strikes Teams are assisting in pollution control efforts in Norfolk and Seattle. We're also using preselected Coast Guard Auxiliarists to augment the Regulars and Reservists as much as possible."

"Admiral, have you augmented your weapons and search packages recently or are you still using the older systems?" queried LaBlanc.

Echoing what Robin has said earlier, Doug answered, "That information is released on a need-to-know basis, and, as of now, I've not been informed you have a need to know."

Flushing angrily, LaBlanc turned to Ann: "That's twice I've been insulted by your subordinates. I was told that I would have access to all information."

"I apologize, Ms. LaBlanc, there wasn't time before the meeting to clarify your access to information to my team. And, in any case, I feel that it would be better done in private since each of us has information that may be too sensitive for general discussion. We can do that after we finish here. Is that acceptable to you?" Ann replied, but she also thought Briggs and Chandler were out of line. She would talk with those two later.

"Thank you, Admiral, that is acceptable," answered LaBlanc. Looking at Doug, LaBlanc gave him a warm smile. "My apologies to you, Captain, I overreacted."

"Ms. Kidd, what have you got for us on logistics?" Ann asked.

The meeting continued for another hour; Kidd and Romanski gave their reports and there was a wide-ranging discussion about the next steps to be undertaken.

"That wraps it up," said Ann. "We'll meet again at two o'clock. Ms. Candler, Captain Briggs, please accompany me to my office. Ms. LaBlanc, I've arranged for you to see the DVD we received, and then would you join us in half an hour?"

All three agreed and the meeting adjourned.

Mark Fletcher had been waiting in the in the hall outside the conference room to see Doug Briggs.

Admiral Gallaher was the first one out, followed by LaBlanc. Mark greeted the admiral, but was caught off guard by the presence of the well-tailored and beautiful civilian behind her.

Seeing the questioning look on Fletcher's face, Ann said: "Ms. LaBlanc, this is Lieutenant Mark Fletcher. As you'll see in the DVD, he's the only person the terrorist will negotiate with."

Before Mark could reply, LaBlanc took the initiative. "Why, Mark, how lovely to see you." she said warmly and gave him a hug.

Taken aback by the unexpected show of warmth, Doug asked: "You two know each other?"

LaBlanc smiled graciously. "We never had the pleasure of meeting."

Mark finally responded, being sure to match LaBlanc's tone. "It's a pleasure to meet you too. I've heard great things about Seiako under your management."

LaBlanc's smile tightened a little at Mark's words. "Thank you, it's nice to know you haven't lost interest in our family's success. And, knowing the Fletchers' history, I'm not surprised you're so deeply involved in this mess. After this is over, we must get together to talk."

"That would be wonderful," Mark replied.

Completely confused by the exchange, Ann asked: "Did you what to see me, Lieutenant?"

"No, Admiral, I had an idea I wanted to discuss with Captain Briggs, but it can wait." And he turned and walked away.

13

U.S. Coast Guard Facilities Center, Galveston, Texas, 8:46 AM (9:46 AM Eastern Time)

Coast Guard Master Chief Boatswains Mate Rich Miller was not a happy camper. Pulling together the Maritime Safety and Security Team (MSST) had gone like clockwork, and the local Coast Guard-led Incident Command System was set up, but not fully operational yet. In addition to the Coast Guard, the FBI, Customs, state police, county sheriff departments, and the local police were getting into the act. On paper everything was set, however, in Miller's opinion, the operation was developing into a major cluster fuck.

The good news was the unit was using the new twenty-five foot, high-speed Defender-class boats. The bad news was that the Defenders' aluminum cabin wasn't armored and the machine gun crews weren't protected by splitter shields.

Some of the unit's boats were equipped with the Integrated Anti-Swimmer System, the underwater anti-diver ultrasound weapons system designed to distinguish humans from marine animals. Under the rules of engagement, however, if a diver was detected, a warning by the underwater loudspeaker would be given. If the warning was ignored, the shockwave emitter would be fired once as a warning, and only if that was ignored could the teams fire to stun or kill. Because they were operating in confined water, the new concussion grenades weren't issued.

Miller figured concussion grenades were the only way to deter swimmers, and the environmental aspects be damned—but it wasn't his call.

USCG Port Security Unit 415, San Pedro, California, 7:00 AM (10:00 AM Eastern Time)

Lieutenant Commander Hank Rodgers, commanding officer of PSU 415, was already tired. A week earlier the unit had returned from a six-month deployment to Iraq and everyone was still trying to readjust to civilian life. More importantly, the unit's boats and weapons needed to be thoroughly overhauled, something that wasn't scheduled to be completed for another month. Now they had less than twenty-four hours to complete the work.

While the crews worked on equipment, Rodgers, as part of the ICS, had been part of a meeting with other agencies and the PACAREA Commander, Vice Admiral Edward Kowosky, to discuss operations.

Everyone—MSSTs, NCWS, Customs, DEA, ATF, and FBI, as well as the state and local agencies—wanted a piece of the action. The Admiral deftly dealt with them all, but it still had been an exhausting meeting.

He'd seen the videos of what happened to the Navy security teams in Norfolk, and, for the first time, realized how vulnerable his crews were. The unit's twenty-five-foot Guardian boats, with their exposed center consoles and three machine-gun mounts, didn't offer any protection from automatic weapons or RPGs. Trying to protect the ports could turn into a suicide mission.

Shaking his head in disgust, Rodgers reached the same conclusion as Master Chief Miller: This was a real cluster fuck.

Coast Guard Headquarters, Washington, D.C., 11:30AM, Eastern Time

Wearily, Ann sank into one of the casual chairs around the coffee table in her office, motioning Candler and Briggs to ones across from her. When they were seated, Ann went on the attack. "What was that need-to-know business you fired at Ms. LaBlanc? She's here at the direction of the President. That was tactless and potentially damaging to any assistance she could provide.

"I know there wasn't time to discuss it beforehand, and I also know you two haven't worked together before. Now, let's hear it. You first, Captain."

Before Doug could answer, Mark burst into the office.

"What in the bloody hell is Evelyn LaBlanc doing here?" he demanded.

Flushing at the outburst, Ann snapped back: "Watch your language, Lieutenant! And stand at attention when you address me."

Ignoring the order, Mark repeated more softly: "What is she doing here?"

"She offered her services as a consultant during the crisis," Ann replied with barely controlled anger.

"And whose bright idea was that?"

Doug stepped in to try to defuse the situation: "She's worked with Secretary Highland before, on matters relating to Homeland Security. Both he and the President thought we should avail ourselves of her generous offer. What do you know about her?"

Mark slumped into a chair. "The LaBlanc family has never done anything that didn't benefit them. They've been involved in every kind of illegal activity you can think of."

"Fletcher, get back on your feet!" snapped Ann. "You've made a serious accusation against Ms. LaBlanc. Can you prove your accusation?"

"I don't have proof. All I know is that they're my family's most implacable enemies. The feud goes back over two hundred years."

"That's nonsense. Feuding died out long ago," said Ann condescendingly. "She runs one of the largest maritime organizations in the world. Why would she care about a feud—if it exists?"

"I don't know," replied Mark, "but the fact that she's involved in this can't be coincidence."

After a brief glance at Robin, which elicited a small shrug, Doug said, "I don't know Ms. LaBlanc and I don't know the real reasons behind her offer. However, there's too much at stake to ignore Fletcher's concerns. Of course I'll obey your orders in this matter, but I'm not comfortable with the situation."

Ann noticed the exchange of looks between Doug and Robin, but ignored it for the moment. Without responding to Doug, she directed Robin to answer the question posed before Mark arrived: "What prompted you to pull the need-to-know nonsense on Ms. LaBlanc?"

Looking directly at Ann, Robin said: "For the same reasons Captain Briggs just gave you. Also, you should know that while it's true Doug and I haven't worked together before, we've shared every other part of our lives for the past six years."

As Ann was trying to absorb this, Doug reached over and squeezed Robin's hand.

"Why wasn't I informed of this?" asked Ann.

"No offence meant, Admiral, but up to now it was none of your damned business," answered Doug, his voice barely under control.

"Offense taken, Captain. Ms. Candler, Captain Briggs, your personal lives are your own. The fact that you are together means I can't be sure I can rely on either of you to arrive at independent conclusions regarding the value of Ms. LaBlanc's contributions. If I could, you would both be replaced, but, unfortunately, there isn't time to do so."

Gallaher moved her focus to Mark. "Fletcher, I think you're being paranoid. Since apparently you're partially responsible for the current crisis, I won't tolerate any further independent actions. Until you can prove your accusations, confine yourself to identifying the terrorist and keep your opinions to yourself. You're dismissed."

Without a word, Mark executed an about face and left the office.

Still not mollified, Ann turned her anger on Doug and Robin. "The same goes for the two of you. There won't be any actions taken regarding Ms. LaBlanc unless I approve them. Is that clear?"

"Yes, Admiral," they replied.

"Good. Now let's see what Ms. LaBlanc has to offer."

Galveston, Texas, 9:00 AM Central Time (11:00 AM Eastern Time)

Just as Lokesh was doing in Los Angeles, Vreeland reconnoitered the target facility. Here, too, additional security was on evidence which, in his professional option, didn't present any unanticipated problems.

The team had flown in over the past week, and each member was staying at a different motel. None of them had left their quarters since Saturday evening. Prior to Sunday's attacks, they had picked up the few needed pieces of specialized equipment before settling in. Waiting for the actual assault to begin, each person checked his or her equipment and hoped there wouldn't be any problems.

14

Coast Guard Headquarters, Washington, D.C., 12:00 PM, Eastern Time

Amy Forrest looked up from her computer as Mark stormed into the office. Still seething over being chewed out, Mark threw himself into the chair at his own desk without a word of greeting.

Ticked off at being ignored, Amy asked: "What's eating at you now?"

"Admiral Gallaher thinks I'm paranoid."

"I think you're crazy, immature, and arrogant. Someone else thinking you're paranoid doesn't surprise me."

"Lieutenant, I don't give a damn what you think," Mark snapped. "What have you got on the terrorist?"

Returning his tone, she replied: "Nothing yet. You didn't give us much to work with. Even the Navy didn't know about your part in the SEAL operation until last night. It really made them look pretty stupid when I began asking questions."

"That's the Navy's problem."

Walking over to his desk, Amy glared down at him. "And now it's mine, thanks to you. Right now you're part of the problem, not part of the solution. So why don't you pipe down and let me get to work since apparently you have nothing else to contribute."

Mark held her gaze for as long as he could before turning back to his computer without another word. The silence stretched for five long minutes. Finally Mark did the hardest thing he'd ever done in his life. He walked over to Amy's desk and squatted down next to her chair.

Wearily she looked at him, ready for anything but what actually happened.

"Amy, I'm sorry," Mark said softly.

She raised an eyebrow. "After chewing me out, you think saying you're sorry makes it all better? You are arrogant."

"I had to try."

As he turned away, Amy asked: "Okay, Fletcher, what's going on?"

"Secretary Highland foisted Evelyn LaBlanc on the ICS as a consultant in maritime security. LaBlanc runs Seiako International, one of the largest shipping companies in the world."

"I don't see anything wrong with that—it makes a lot of sense."

"It would to me too, if her family and mine hadn't been at war with each other for a couple of centuries."

"That's crazy," said Amy. "Is that why Admiral Gallaher thinks you're paranoid?"

This time, instead of losing his temper, Mark pulled his desk chair over next to Amy and carefully explained the situation.

It had all started when one of his ancestors stopped a LaBlanc from massacring the passengers and crew of a merchant ship during the Revolutionary War.

"That's a long time ago, Mark."

"Yeah, but the LaBlancs have been involved with slavery, drug smuggling, weapons deals, and piracy ever since."

"How do you know?"

"My father intercepted one of their drug and slave shipments during Vietnam. Evelyn's brother, Eric, was there."

"What happened?"

"Eric shot at my dad and missed. My dad shot back and didn't."

Amy sat back in her chair. "Wow. That would be reason enough to want you dead, but why wait so long?"

"Because the LaBlancs always combine business with pleasure. There's something else going on behind the attacks that I'm not seeing."

Amy sat quietly for a moment, her mind moving through all the angles of the bigger picture she could see. "Based on what you've told me, I agree with your judgment of Evelyn LaBlanc. I don't believe in coincidence and her offer is too timely." She looked him squarely in the eyes. "How do we handle this?"

Fletcher smiled, relieved she believed him. "Very carefully. First, we identify the largest maritime forwarding companies, and also look for companies who control port operations. Once we have those names, we look into their operations over the past three years. Specifically, we look for any financial troubles, efforts to expand their US facilities, evidence or rumors of take-over attempts, and anything else that doesn't fit a normal pattern."

"Okay, but why?"

"Because U.S. companies are not in the top ranks of global terminal operators. Terminal operations are now controlled primarily by Terra Marine in Hong Kong, PSA in Singapore and Dubai Ports World. There are a handful of others, but none have the resources of those three." He remembered something. "A couple of years ago there was something suspicious about the sale of Peninsular & Oriental Steam Navigation to Dubai. I couldn't put my finger on it then, and that might be a good place to start now."

Forrest was taking a few notes, nodding. "That makes sense and I'll get going on it. What about you?"

"I'm still trying to find out who ran the ambush in Iraq. While I'm waiting for answers, I'll start looking into LaBlanc's connection to Highland." He looked into her eyes. "Amy, we have to be very careful not to set off any alarms."

"I know, Mark. I get it, really."

Gently touching Amy's hand with his fingertips, Mark said: "Amy, I mean very careful. If there's something deeper, and LaBlanc finds out we know about it, she'll have us killed."

Surprised by the gesture, Amy looked up to see a caring look in Mark's eyes as he said,

"You're a remarkable person and I'm glad we're working together."

"Thanks a lot Mark, but next time get someone else to watch your back" she answered frostily.

15

Los Angeles, California, 9:30 AM (12:30 PM Eastern Time)
Lokesh drove along the docks. At each terminal, extra security guards were in evidence. Although armed, none looked too impressive. As expected there were an increased number of armed patrol boats in the harbor, and military helicopters crisscrossed the sky.

His team was resting after the Seattle attack. All had gone as planned: The six men reached the rendezvous without incident, and there were no reports of them having been seen. Reaching the airport within an hour of the attacks, they boarded their chosen flights without any trouble. Again, careful planning had minimized the risk—all the round-trip tickets were purchased more than three weeks in advance.

Upon returning from the reconnaissance, Akbar met him with a questioning look.

"It still looks good, but we'll check again this evening. It will matter little how thorough their patrols are. By using the self-contained rebreathing units, there won't be any bubbles."

"Yes," agreed Akbar, "but if they drop concussion grenades, we're going to be fish food. Underwater the shockwaves will turn our insides to mush."

"We can't count on that not happening, but the Americans are so concerned about their environment, I don't think we need to be worried," countered Lokesh. "Now, are the escape vehicles in place?"

"I checked this morning and they're ready when we need them. I fear this attack will be costly to us, no matter how careful we are."

"What did you expect?" asked Lokesh. "That, as the Americans say, is why we make the big bucks. Now, my friend, let's talk with our comrades once more. We will say nothing of our fears."

Coast Guard Headquarters, Washington, D.C., 2:00PM

When everyone was seated for the third ICS meeting, Ann asked Robin Candler for her report.

"No progress as yet in identifying the terrorist leader, but we've extended our search to Iraq since that incident is the only link we know of with Fletcher. We've been more successful in finding out about the suicide boat crews. There've been several calls from the Virginia Beach area from people who recently sold the types of boats used in the attack. One was able to give us a good description of a couple who bought his boat. This description was passed to the local law-enforcement agencies, and they're canvassing the area to find out where they lived and any known associates. So far, they've drawn a blank, but it's early in the process.

"We have positively identified the owners of the cabin cruiser used as a decoy. It belonged to Mr. and Mrs. Henry Williams. According to neighbors, the Williamses had left that morning for a cruise up the Chesapeake and weren't expected back for several weeks."

"Who knew about their plans?" asked Ken James.

"A number of their friends in the neighborhood, and their plans had been talked about around the marina. The police checked at the marina, and no one there remembers anyone paying particular attention to the Williamses."

"Are there security cameras at the marina?" LaBlanc wanted to know.

"No, there aren't. Access to the docks is controlled by locked gates with bright lights mounted on poles along each of the docks. They haven't had any thefts in over five years, so the security appeared adequate."

"Not good news, but thanks," said Ann. Then she addressed the whole group. "Do you think the terrorists will use suicide boats again? We'll begin with the most junior member, Jon Romanski."

"Admiral, as you know, this isn't my area of expertise."

"I know, but I want your gut reaction."

Pausing for a moment to collect his thoughts, Jon answered: "I don't think so. They must know we'll be ready for this type of attack. As we've learned, terrorist leaders are usually not stupid."

Commander Julia Kidd interjected, "I agree with Jon. The terrorists may be counting on us looking for other types of attacks, and then use the same scenario again—-but I don't think so."

Ann turned to Robin: "What's your take on this?"

"My evaluation is the same Jon's and Julia's. We have to look at other options."

Without waiting, Ken James and Doug Briggs added their voices, backing the concept that the terrorists wouldn't repeat themselves.

The final opinion heard was LaBlanc's. "There's nothing in my experience that allows for any other conclusion."

"I'll make it unanimous," was all Ann said before LaBlanc interrupted.

"Excuse me, Admiral, may I ask what the members feel are the likely methods to be used in the next attack?"

"That's a good question, but we'll table it for the moment, Ms. LaBlanc," Ann replied. "Admiral James, how's the DOG doing?"

LaBlanc held back her displeasure, and didn't raise the question again. She did make several suggestions regarding acquiring additional security from private firms, and recapped her initial work toward gathering intelligence from her personal international network.

Having learned that any direct request for operational information would either be refused or tactfully ignored, LaBlanc was still able to glean what she wanted to know from James's briefing and Candler's information about the Iraqi connection.

The next meeting was scheduled for nine-thirty the following morning, thirty minutes before the terrorist's deadline. Before then LaBlanc had much to do.

Coast Guard Headquarters, 4:30 PM, Eastern Time
"Got a minute?"

Robin looked up from the report she was reading to see Amy Forrest standing in the office doorway. "Sure, come in."

After taking a seat, Amy began. "I've located all the SEAL team members that Fletcher was with. The CNO had his aide call each SEAL and arrange for them to be brought here by tomorrow morning. Also, I've got the eyewitness who saw the men escape from the fishing boat in Seattle."

"Good work, but you didn't just come over to tell me that, right?"

"No," said Amy, handing Robin two pieces of paper. "Take a look at the name of the eyewitness and the names of the SEALs."

After looking at the names, Robin asked, "Have you told Mark yet?"

"No, I wanted to tell you first. The witness's wife was killed in the attack. I feel you and Captain Briggs should meet him before Mark comes in."

"Good work. I'll call Admiral Gallaher right now and let her know. When the witness gets here, show him the DVD, and then the two of you should come to my office."

"Thanks, Robin. I'll see you later."

16

Coast Guard Pacific Area Headquarters, Oakland, California, 3:30 PM (6:30 PM Eastern Time)

Vice Admiral Jessie Veath, Pacific Area Commander, entered the conference room and took his place at the head of the table. Assembled were the members of his staff, and conferenced-in by phone were the commanding officers of the Marine Safety and Security Teams, Port Security Units, and the cutters assigned to harbor security, along with their respective executive officers and senior petty officers.

"We ready to go?" he asked. After receiving affirmatives, he began. "Have each of you seen the Commandant's order regarding courses of action?"

There was another round of affirmatives.

"Good, there's a lot to be done quickly. Also, I want to hear any ideas any of you have for additional security measures and personnel safety."

Lieutenant Commander John Quigley, Commanding Officer of the San Diego-based MSST, was the first to respond. "With all due respect, Admiral, headquarters is over-reacting.

My team's been deployed in the Los Angeles area for four days, and we haven't seen or heard any unusual activity. The local law-enforcement agencies haven't come up with anything either. I don't believe the terrorists will strike there; San Diego is more likely. We're well-trained to defend both the facilities and ourselves, and I resent some desk jockey dictating that we change our procedures on short notice."

"He's got a point, Admiral," added Commander Levensian, Commanding Officer of the 270-foot cutter *Corwin*. "I don't know how Captain Briggs came up with some of this. It sounds to me like he's been reading too many bad novels. Also, the orders substantially alter the Coast Guard's use-of-force policy, something the Commandant can't do without approval from a higher authority."

Keeping his thoughts to himself about their comments, Veath asked, "Anyone else have objections or comments about these issues?"

Emboldened by the words of two senior commanding officers, the lieutenant commanding the 110-foot cutter *Paddocks Island* and the chief petty officer in charge of the 87-foot cutter *Trigger Fish* said they felt the same way. Headquarters was wrong, and what they were expected to do went against the grain; they considered themselves shepherds, not hunters.

Veath replied, "I respect your opinions, but I'll remind you that this situation is not precedent-setting. During the Rum Wars in the 1920s, during World War II, and in Vietnam, the Coast Guard used force preemptively to stop the enemy."

"You've all seen what happened in Norfolk and Seattle. Do you think this group will hesitate to shoot?"

Levensian spoke up again. "That's all well and good, Admiral, but it doesn't change my feelings on this matter, and I don't believe that the Commandant's orders are lawful."

Flushed from the Admiral's open rebuke, Quigley backed Levensian.

Veath had considered there might be objections to the orders, and, to that end, had had a long discussion with Vince Story, Ann Gallaher and Vice Admiral Audrey Stuart, Coast Guard Atlantic Area Commander. They all agreed that extreme situations called for extreme measures. The hardest decision they made was that any commanding officer who balked when ordered to act aggressively was to be relieved of his or her command immediately. There wasn't time for the niceties of doing it in the traditional manner. Each admiral knew, and was willing to accept, the consequences of such actions.

"Are each of you refusing to carry out the Commandant's orders?" he asked in a somber tone.

Each of the four replied that he or she would comply with all lawful orders, but did not believe this constituted such an order.

"Then it is my duty to relieve each of you immediately, and assign you to my staff until otherwise directed by the Commandant. You will report to my office within six hours, and are further ordered not to discuss the circumstance of your relief to anyone prior to arriving here. Your respective executive officers will assume command of your unit until otherwise directed."

Stunned, two of the four commanding officers mumbled, "Aye, aye, Admiral."

Levensian's anger flared up. "You can't do this! I'll file charges against you and the Commandant."

"Commander, you can file whatever charges you wish after you report as ordered. Right now, you are relieved and will report to this office," answered Veath, more calmly than he felt. "Do you understand?"

Incensed, Quigley asked, "What happens if we don't?"

"You will be placed under arrest and confined to the brig. What's your decision?"

Quigley's face turned ashen at the thought of being arrested. "I'll report to your office as ordered."

"Commander Levensian, what's your decision?"

"I'll comply with your orders, under protest."

With that, the four now former commanding officers withdrew.

Saddened by the necessity of his actions, Veath turned back to the main purpose of the meeting.

The Jefferson Hotel Presidential Suite, Washington, D.C., 7:00 PM Eastern Time

Evelyn LaBlanc was deep in thought as she entered the suite.

Gwen looked up from her work. Seeing the look on her boss's face, she went to the bar and poured two glasses of vodka.

Handling one to LaBlanc, who had settled on the couch, Goldin asked: "What's the matter?"

"Not a thing. Gallaher and her crew are doing exactly what we planned on. I need to talk to the Russian so we can get the information out to our Middle-Eastern friend."

Goldin went to the desk, selected a cell phone from among several, and passed it to LaBlanc. As usual, the call was short and the conversation carefully worded. When it ended, LaBlanc filled Goldin in on the day's meetings, including the unexpected one with Fletcher.

"Interesting," said Goldin. "And what's Highland doing?"

"He's using his contacts to keep track of Gallagher's intelligence queries. And, for right now, keeping a low profile as instructed. Now, bring me up to date on our investments, and then we'll decide where to have dinner."

17

TUESDAY

Galveston, Texas, 2:00 AM (4:00 AM Eastern Time)
"The best way to hide something is in plain sight," Vreeland thought as he drove a van emblazoned with the name of a well-known security firm toward the docks. Cruising slowly into the target area, the right rear door slid open, and, one by one, the team members jumped out, carrying their rebreather units and knives. Moving with practiced ease, they slipped past the patrolling guards at the container facility, and each paused briefly at the pier edge to don a rebreather unit before slipping into the water.

Once in the water, the team submerged. Even though the rebreathing units didn't leave a trail of bubbles, they wove their way through the pilings where no one could see them. The murky water was ghostly, lit only by light from the piers overhead. Retrieving the packages emplaced weeks before, the divers moved along a ship's hull, attaching limpet mines every fifty feet. When all the charges were in place and the timers set, they ditched their diving gear and climbed onto the pier.

From there it was easy to slip over the ship's shadowed stern. After posting two lookouts, the other four moved along the deck, stopping only to set more charges. Their work completed, the team reassembled and, as briefed, they moved to two empty cabins. Safely out of sight, the group made themselves comfortable; it would be some time before the assault.

Los Angeles, California, 3:00 AM (6:00 AM Eastern Time)

Using the same scenario as Vreeland, Lokesh dropped off his team and headed back to the warehouse. Abandoning the van, he got into a rental car and headed for the work boat. It was essential to be in place before the attack began.

Keeping to the outside of the facility's chain-link fence, Lokesh's team eased toward the water's edge. Tens yards from their goal, a guard's flashlight slashed through the shadows. Everyone froze. Akbar, who was just outside the light's cone, reached down and gently pulled his knife out. From the light's backwash he saw there were two guards standing close together, each carrying a lightweight assault rifle slung over his shoulder.

"Amateurs," Akbar thought derisively, hoping they would decide they were seeing things and go away. Tense seconds passed as they talked, trying to decide whether or not to investigate further.

He heard them call the report in, then, unslinging weapons, they moved in. As the guards moved forward, Akbar slipped further to their left, working his way around behind them. Out of the corner of his eye, he saw his fellow team member Ishmael moving around to the right. Stopping five yards from the team, one of the guards called out: "We see you! Stand up with your hands over your head or we'll shoot!"

Slowly, the one man and three women obeyed the command, focusing attention away from the two moving up behind the unsuspecting guards. To ensure they had the guards' undivided attention, the women slowly stripped open their vests to reveal unfettered breasts. It was the last thing either guard saw as razor-sharp knives were thrust up through their jaws.

As the women closed their vests, the men carried the two bodies to the edge of the pier.

Knowing the guards would soon be missed, Akbar told the team to get into the water, taking the bodies with them.

The ringing phone surprised Lokesh; there weren't to be any calls until the attack was over. This could only mean trouble.

"What's wrong?" he asked, and listened as Akbar explained what had happened.

Lokesh remained cool. "Continue as planned. Just make sure you're well concealed since they'll search thoroughly for intruders. If they don't find anyone, the ship will still sail on schedule."

Akbar heard the sound of rapidly-approaching vehicles as he joined the team already in the water. By the time vehicles arrived, the team had sunk the bodies between the ship and the pier and begun attaching the limpet mines as planned.

Scott Jacobs, the head of security, was trying to find out what happened. Two of his men were missing after calling in a suspicious sighting. Arriving on the scene, there was no sign of the men or any indication of a struggle.

Jacobs told his assistant: "Secure the area, then call the police. Tell them we've lost two guards under suspicious circumstances. Also notify the Coast Guard and see if they can sweep the area for swimmers. The *Nordic Star* is due to sail in seven hours. I want her searched, and station armed guards at the pilot house and assign roving patrols to the decks."

His assistant protested that Jacobs didn't have the authority to put armed men on the ship.

"Just do it for now. I'll see if the Coast Guard can spare us some people to take over when the ship sails."

Over the next hour, his level of frustration and concern increased as negative reports came in from the search teams. By the time the Coast Guard arrived, the intruders were nowhere to be found. The Coast Guard dispatched a boat with the integrated anti-swimmer system to investigate the immediate area. After using the unit's sonar to determine there weren't any swimmers in the area, the crew deployed the robotic cameras to check the ship's hull.

The limpets were placed on the ship's side facing the pier and were not seen.

Los Angeles, California, 5:00 AM (8:00 AM Eastern Time)

Lieutenant Hank Rodgers, the recently promoted Commanding Officer of the San Diego Marine Safety and Security Team, was going over the team's final deployments when someone called: "Attention on Deck."

Annoyed at being interrupted, he looked around to see Lieutenant Commander John Quigley, who, until yesterday, had been his commanding officer. Very formally, he said: "Good morning, Commander. What may I do for you?"

"Good morning, Lieutenant. May I see you privately for a moment?"

The request made Hank uncomfortable. He knew Quigley had no business there, and, in fact, was supposed to be at Pacific Area headquarters in Oakland by now. But they had worked together for a long time, so he granted Quigley's request.

To his staff, he said, "I'll be right back." To Quigley, "This way, please, Commander," and went into a small room.

When the door was closed, he turned on him sharply.

"You're not supposed to be here. You're AWOL, and I should at least report your presence, if not arrest you. But you know all that. What do want, John?"

"Yeah, Hank, I know I'm putting you on the spot by being here, and I'm sorry," he replied.

Hank softened his tone. "Why are you here and, again, what do you want?"

"I want to ride one of the boats as crew, and I want the chance to prove my estimation of the situation is the correct one. My career's in the tank, so it doesn't matter one way or the other if I'm AWOL on top of everything else."

Hank thought over what he was asking. They were long-time friends, and had, together, built the team. Sometimes the conflicting pull between loyalty, friendship, duty, and the chain-of-command got in the way. When that happened, you needed to do the best you could and usually go with your gut reaction.

Hank's duty was to arrest Quigley for disobeying orders—but his gut reaction was to put Quigley on a boat. The team was short a gunner, and Quigley was good with the weapons. No matter what he did, Hank was headed for trouble.

"Okay, take the .50 caliber machine gun on Number 4 boat. I'll tell the coxswain what's going on."

"Thanks, Hank."

"One more thing: You're a gunner, not the coxswain, so don't take try to take over. Got it?"

"Aye, aye, Lieutenant," Quigley replied, "and thanks again."

18

Coast Guard Headquarters, 7:30 AM Eastern Time
Ann was just entering her austerely furnished office when the phone started ringing. She grabbed the handset.

"Gallaher."

"Admiral, this is Commander Long, Communication Duty Officer. There's been an incident at a container facility in Los Angeles. At approximately 3:15 local time, two guards disappeared after calling in a suspicious sighting."

"What are the details and what actions have been taken?" Ann asked.

When the report was finished, she asked Long to get in touch with the ICS team and have them assemble at 8:30.

The Jefferson Hotel Presidential Suite, Washington, D.C., 7:45 AM
Gwen entered the bathroom with a cup of cappuccino as Evelyn LaBlanc stepped out of the shower.

"Gallaher just called," Gwen said. "She wants the ICS team assembled by 8:30."

"What's going on?"

"There's been a report that two guards disappeared at a container terminal in LA early this morning. A thorough search of the area didn't turn up either the guards or any solid evidence of terrorist activity, but Gallaher pushed the panic button," Gwen replied. Anticipating the next question, she continued: "I haven't heard from al-Hishma or Demivov, so either they're keeping it to themselves or haven't been informed by the team leader."

As she was drying her hair, LaBlanc thought what impact the foul-up would have on the operation. Through Gwen, she had dossiers on all of al-Hishma's team members. Lokesh was a good choice and his team was the better of the two.

Finishing her toilette and beginning to dress, LaBlanc asked Gwen: "What's your evaluation of the report?"

"I think we're okay. Everyone on the ICS team believes there'll be more attacks. The media is having a field day looking for terrorists everywhere, confusing the situation with useless advice, and generally keeping the public in a low state of panic. As usual, the politicians are pointing out how they would handle the crisis, and they're too busy forming investigative committees to add anything constructive."

"I agree. Call Highland and have his media people leak news of the LA incident to the press. Follow up with our own contacts; I want this out there just before the next attacks." Looking in to the mirror for a final check, she added with a smile, "It's time for Highland to become more visible.

Coast Guard Headquarters, 9:45 AM Eastern Time

After reviewing the information from LA, including talks with Jacobs and Rodgers, the members of the ICS team agreed this indicated another attack was in the works.

The Deployable Operation Group's CO, Ken James, summed up their conclusions.

"We assumed there would be other, coordinated attacks. Based on the report from LA, let's work on the principle that at least one East or Gulf Coast facility has been infiltrated. There are too many for each one to be searched by the deadline, and even if we could get to them all, we're not sure what we're looking for. The consensus is that the terrorist won't use suicide boats again, but will attempt to take over one of the outbound ships.

"To counter that threat, we've dispatched security teams to as many outbound ships as we can within the time frame. Commander Rodgers already has one on board *Nordic Star*, which is the only West Coast ship I think we need to cover."

LaBlanc asked: "Do you think the presence of armed teams will dissuade the terrorists? After all, we're dealing with fanatics."

"Ms. LaBlanc, our teams are all well-trained professionals, and certainly a match for any fanatics."

"I'm sure you're right, Admiral, thank you," LaBlanc said, giving the admiral a warm smile, knowing he and his teams would soon see some real professionals at work.

Doug Briggs thought they were missing something important, but couldn't put his finger on it. Looking at Robin, he saw that she, too, was troubled. What could it be? Time was rapidly running out.

Limpet mines? But swimmers couldn't get past the anti-swimmer system—or could they? A classic military failure is underestimating your enemy. If they were smart enough to figure out the choke points, something as simple as the anti-swimmer system's weak points wouldn't have been missed. And it was obvious concussion grenades weren't being used.

"Admiral James, how thoroughly was the hull swept?"

"I covered that. According to Commander Rodgers, every foot of the eight-hundred-foot hull, both port and starboard, was gone over by the robot camera. Optic conditions weren't the best, but I'm satisfied Rodger's people did a good job."

"How far below the waterline was the search?"

"From waterline down to five feet—that's the camera's range in a single sweep."

Before Doug could formulate another question, the phone rang.

Time had run out.

"Admiral Gallaher, this is the switchboard. There's a man on the line asking for Lieutenant Fletcher. Should I put him through?"

"Yes, transfer him to me, and then please ask Lieutenant Fletcher to join me," replied Ann. When the phone rang again, Ann hit the speaker button. "This is Admiral Gallaher. Fletcher will be here in a moment."

A voice grated through the speaker, "You did not ask who was calling."

"That would have been a stupid question," Ann shot back as Mark entered the conference room.

"I did not expect such an intelligent response from a woman. Now get off the phone and let me speak to Fletcher."

"I'm here," said Mark. "What is it that you want to know?"

"Are you going to meet my demands?"

Mark looked at Ann before replying. The decision had been made, but he wanted a last confirmation. Ann shook her head.

"Killing hundreds of people and then demanding money is blackmail. The United States does not pay blackmail."

"It is not blackmail. There are two lessons you must learn, and the deaths are the cost of your first lesson."

"Two lessons? Your attacks have to do with lessons?" asked Mark.

"Yes, the first lesson is that no nation can turn its back while thousands are murdered without getting soaked in their blood."

Mark responded, "No one is innocent when another is slain. That's a lesson we all know, so you've killed in vain and won't be allowed to profit from it."

"Each lesson has its own cost. You have paid for the first; the money is the cost of the second lesson."

"What is the second lesson?" Marked asked, fearing the answer.

"It is simple: Do only that which is yours to do, and stay out of matters that are not your concern. The consequences of such action could well reach farther than you imagine. It is a lesson for your country, and for you personally, Mark Fletcher."

"I don't understand. What has my country, and, more specifically, what have I done that we should not have?"

"Pay the price and you will find out."

"No," said Mark, "I, we will not. We know about the team in Los Angeles. Call them off and we can talk further."

"The knowing will do you no good. Now, if you will not pay in cash and deed, then payment will be extracted another way. I will call again in two days to see if you have changed your mind."

The dial tone terminated the conversation.

19

Los Angeles, California, 7:10 AM (10:10 AM Eastern Time)

Helped by the outgoing tide, the container ship *Nordic Star* made her way toward the breakwater. Once past that, she would be on her way to Hong Kong via Honolulu. From the Bridge, armed Coast Guard boats, with machine guns manned and ready, were visible. Along her deck patrolled more armed Coast Guard personnel

Captain van Skyler, *Nordic Star's* captain, said: "I'm glad we're leaving and not coming in. Once clear, there's nothing to worry about but the weather. "

Hugh Samcoski, the harbor pilot, was nodding his head in agreement when explosions ripped out the whole right side of the ship ten feet below the waterline. As the last one died away, Vincent and van Skyler rushed out and looked over the side. Torrents of water poured through the shattered hull, pulling the ship over.

Samcoski stood momentarily speechless as van Skyler grabbed the microphone for the ship's PA system: "This is the captain, all hands abandon ship, all hands abandon ship."

There was no need to radio a MAYDAY call; every other ship and boat in the harbor had heard the explosions and could see the *Nordic Star* heeling over. Drifting towards the breakwater, she swung broadside to the opening, containers cascading from her deck.

Galveston, Texas, 9:15 AM (10:15 AM Eastern Time)

BMCM Rich Miller was at the helm of an armed twenty-two-foot boat patrolling the lower end of Galveston Harbor, his three gunners scanning the area for any unusual activity. Everyone was on edge; they had all seen what happened in Norfolk and Seattle. Miller noticed the *Evangeline*, an outbound container ship, was almost to the breakwater, and he turned to make one final sweep around her.

"Oh my god!" hollered one of his gunners.

Miller saw a sheet of fire rippling along the *Evangeline*'s hull. "Get down!" he shouted, spinning the boat away from the wall of water thrown up by the explosions surging toward him. Pieces of white-hot metal rained down, smashing the gunwales and hitting the hull.

From the bow came a cry: "I'm hit! I'm hit!"

Miller turned to the two gunners behind him. "Saad, go forward and take care of Dakota. Yoblonski, check the guns for damage, we may need them."

"Aye, aye, Chief," came the instant replies.

Reaching Dakota, Saad saw he had a bad burn on his neck and a gash in his left leg. She cleaned and bandaged the leg first, then put salve on the burn.

"You okay now?" she asked.

"Yeah, thanks."

"Good, now check your weapon and let's get to work," Saad replied and headed back to her own machine gun.

Under his breath, Dakota said: "Hard-nosed witch. She's as tough as the chief."

Seeing that his crew was still 100 percent operational, Miller headed back to the burning, listing ship.

Coast Guard Headquarters, 10:20 AM, Eastern Time

The discussion regarding the call was getting heated when: "Admiral, this is the Comms Center. They've struck in LA and Galveston."

As the report continued, Doug turned on the multiple flat-panel screens mounted on the walls. Some of these he tuned to various television stations while others connected directly to the LANTAREA and PACAREA ICS conference rooms. As he was involved in this, the Commandant walked in unobtrusively and sat down next to Ann Gallaher.

There was a constant stream of new information being relayed as soon as it was received.

Ann started the meeting. "I want your gut reactions to these attacks, keeping in mind that the first and only call we've had from the terrorist leader ended only ten minutes before they began. We'll start with the most junior member in rank. That's you, Fletcher."

"We were set up. From what we know, there's no way they could have cancelled the attack. Those charges had to be set hours earlier. They had to know ahead of time we wouldn't pay."

Ann asked, "Robin, what's your take on this?"

"I agree with Fletcher. It's too soon and too well-orchestrated. I think there's something or someone working at a deeper level, inside our own operation."

Before anyone could respond, a grim voice from the Comms Center broke in: "Admiral, we've just had more reports."

"Go ahead," said Ann, "what have you got?"

Los Angeles, California, 7:30 AM (10:30 AM Eastern Time)

The area around the *Nordic Star* was chaotic, with boats converging on the scene, weaving through containers floating in the water, and the ship's crew trying to get off. A pleasure boat had just reached some of the men when the container next to them blew up, obliterating the rescuers and the rescued.

Grabbing his radio, van Skyler called over the emergency channel: "They've booby-trapped the cargo. Everybody clear the area now!"

Helplessly he watched other containers explode. Boats were colliding as they scrambled to get clear, adding to the maelstrom of fire and smoke. With a grinding crash, the ship and breakwater met, knocking Van Skyler off his feet. As he went to check on Vincent and the helmsman, van Skyler heard gunfire coming from behind him.

"What now?" asked Vincent.

The helmsman saw it first. "Someone's firing on the rescue boats!" he called. "Why isn't the Coast Guard shooting back?"

"They can't angle their guns high enough," replied Vincent.

Helplessly they watched as six figures obliterated the onboard Coast Guard security in a few seconds. A terrorist gunner spotted the trio on the bridge and fired a burst. The bullets easily cleaved the metal in front of the three witnesses; jagged shards sliced their unprotected clothes and flesh.

Los Angeles Harbor, 7:25 AM (10:25 AM Eastern Time)

MSST Boat #4 was cruising near the breakwater when the coxswain, BM2 Sara Wang heard, "All units, this is Coach, message follows: Tango Alpha execute, repeat Tango Alpha execute."

"This is it, people. Keep your eyes peeled," she called to the gunners. Sweeping the area around her patrol area, Wang didn't see anything unusual. It had been a quiet morning; the only disconcerting thing was having her former CO assigned as a gunner, but, so far, everything was cool.

As Sara swung the boat back on another leg, a message came over the radio. "All units, this is Coach. Tangos may be on board outbound ships. If you see armed personnel on board a ship who are not Coast Guard, you are to fire immediately. End message."

Wang called: "Okay, everybody, load your weapons."

At the forward gun, Lieutenant Commander Quigley was surprised that authorization to use their weapons had been given so soon and without any apparent threat.

"What's going on?" he wondered aloud as he chambered a round in the fifty-caliber machine gun, checking to see if the ammunition belt was clear. Quigley looked up as the first limpet exploded.

Wang, seeing the rippling explosions, radioed, "Coach, this is Left end, a pass is in the air near the End Zone. We're moving to intercept. Request assistance. Over."

"Left end, this is Coach. Roger, Free Safeties and Tackles are on their way."

"Tell them to hurry, it's a bullet pass," Sara finished, pushing the boat up to full speed and angling towards the target. When they were a hundred yards away, figures appeared on the ship's bridge, waving frantically.

Quigley yelled: "Looks like they're friendly."

"Shut up, Commander," snapped Wang. "Keep your eyes on the target and your thoughts to yourself."

Forgetting his promise to Rodgers, Quigley barked back, "Who are you giving orders to?" He left his gun and was headed towards Wang at the control console when a blow smacked him to the deck. Momentarily stunned, Quigley lay there as the rest of the burst sprayed through the hull and ricocheted off the console's armor.

Ears ringing from the blow, he heard the aft machine guns open fire. Just as Quigley was struggling to his feet, a hand spun him around and delivered a jarring slap across his face.

"Get back to your gun, you stupid bastard!" shouted Wang. "If you leave your station again, I'll shoot you myself."

Shocked more by the words than the blow, Quigley stumbled to his gun and opened fire.

As bullets sang their deadly song all around the boat, a grim-faced twenty-one-year-old Sara Wang wove a zigzag course toward the container ship, all the while praying that none of her crew would be killed.

Two armed helicopters roared overhead and a 110-foot cutter closed in.

A badly shaken John Quigley watched miniature waterspouts from the bullets walk towards the boat. Shaking off his shock, he grabbed the machine gun and sent a fiery line of bullets and tracers sweeping upward toward the enemy.

Just before reaching its target, the gun jammed. As he reached for the cocking lever to clear it, a searing pain ripped through his left arm. Quigley saw a jagged piece of steel had shattered his elbow, shredding the surrounding arteries and veins.

Screaming with rage and frustration, he savagely yanked the lever back with his right hand, cleared the jam and pulled the trigger. Throwing his weight against the gun, Quigley continued the traverse, seeming to catch the terrorist as he ducked below the rail. Quigley released the trigger and collapsed, dead before his body hit the deck, unaware that he'd missed.

Standing on *Nordic Star*'s listing deck, Akbar called to his companions: "We are done here. Let us take our departure." Weapons were pitched over the side; ropes were lowered to the water, and, once again, the attackers slipped away.

Galveston, Texas, 8:30 AM (10:30 AM Eastern Time)

As he approached the *Evangeline*, Miller noticed several people on her deck, frantically waving.

"There's crew still on board," he radioed to his base. "We'll try to get them."

Just as he pulled beneath where they were standing, gunfire ripped into the boat. Shoving the throttles wide open, Miller peeled away and barked: "Open fire, open fire."

Only one machine gun lashed back, and that one couldn't be elevated high enough to hit the enemy standing above them. Frantically Miller zigzagged through the containers surrounding him, trying to get away. Bullets ripped up the stern, tearing a hole in the hull, shredding the cover over the console, and pounding into Miller' body armor. A round smashed his shoulder.

Finally, when they cleared out of range, Miller called out, "Everybody okay?"

Silence was the only reply. Risking a look over his shoulder, he saw what was left of Saad and Yoblonski lying next to their useless, unshielded guns.

Trying to control the bile rising in his throat, he yelled: "Dakota, answer up." Slowing to a stop, Miller painfully made his way forward. A swath of blood leading from the gun over the side was the only trace left of Dakota.

Collapsing onto the flooding deck, Miller didn't hear the pulsating sirens of approaching rescue boats or notice as containers began exploding around him.

Los Angels, California, 7:30 AM (10:30 AM Eastern Time)

Unnoticed in the chaos, the work boat wove around the outer edge, apparently looking for survivors. Locating a group, it stopped to take them on board.

"Did you enjoy your swim?" he asked Akbar. When the whole group had arrived, he complimented them. "You did well. We are now halfway there. Let us celebrate quietly tonight before we prepare for our next assignment."

With that, he motioned them below decks and headed towards the piers, blending easily into the mass of traffic around him.

20

Coast Guard Headquarters, 10:35AM, Eastern Time
The reports came in an unbroken stream.

LANTAREA's input: "Terrorists on the ships are strafing the MSST and rescue boats with automatic weapons. Also, some of the containers in the water are exploding. Indications are that they have been booby-trapped. We don't have any word on casualties yet."

PACAREA reported the same thing.

The reports served as commentary to the images from media helicopters being shown on the room's monitors.

"Thank you," said an ashen-faced Ann. Robin stifled a sob, her shoulders shaking with grief and anger. Briggs, Fletcher, and James fought to control their mounting rage while LaBlanc showed no emotion at all.

Vince Story watched and listened without comment, then leaned over to Ann and said softly: "Ann, I need to see you outside for a moment."

She looked around to see the admiral heading for the conference door. Apparently no one else had noticed the commandant's arrival or departure.

Standing up, she said: "Let's start evaluating the impact of these attacks. Admiral James, work on the DOG's losses. Ms. Chandler, get in touch with the CNO and Army Chief of Staff and his people about any anticipated disruptions in supplies to Iraq. Captain Briggs, you and Fletcher review the terrorist's conversation. Ms. LaBlanc, please use your sources to evaluate the impact on other US port operations. I'll be back in a few minutes."

Although puzzled by Gallaher's departure at this critical time, the team immediately focused on their respective assignments.

Vince Story was leaning against the wall in the hall when Ann came out.

"What's gong on, Admiral?" she asked.

"Let's go to my office and I'll tell you."

Once there and settled, Story told her: "Highland called me and said he wants you replaced as head of the ICS handling this. Right after he hung up, another call came in from the Chairman of the Appropriations Committee, and he, too, wants you removed."

Stunned, Ann asked: "Did they give any reasons? Did they make any suggestions as to my replacement?"

"The answer to both is no—but I probably should say not yet. They've asked me for suggestions. And Highland's scheduled a press conference later this morning to make his request public."

"Does this come from the President or is it Highland's idea?"

"I don't know. I placed a call to him, but haven't heard back."

"What are you going to do?"

"Nothing except keep you in place. You're doing a good job."

"How about the political pressure?"

"I'm not vulnerable to that, so don't be concerned. Highland's been against you from the beginning, and this crisis is a good opportunity to prove he was right. It's also a path to national prominence for him. There's more going on here than meets the eye."

Story's last comment gave her pause. Vince had been a friend for a long time, and his insights into situations were always on the mark. "Vince, Fletcher blew up after he met Evelyn LaBlanc and mentioned a feud between his family and the LaBlancs. I dismissed it as paranoia on his part. Is that something you're aware of?"

"No, but whatever else he is, Mark Fletcher isn't paranoid. Maybe we need to take a closer look at Evelyn LaBlanc's relationship with Highland," replied Story, unaware Forrest was already doing just that. "Now, go back and see if we can stop the terrorist before he strikes again. I'll keep the heat off you."

Galveston, Texas, 8:45 AM (10:45 AM Eastern Time)

An Emergency Response team truck drove slowly along the breakwater, the driver searching for survivors of the attack. He stopped near where six people were climbing up the rocks. Getting out, he opened the back doors, then went down to assist them.

"*Muy bien*, very good," said Vreeland to his team, "but hurry. We have to get out of here before anyone else comes." When everyone was in, he started back down the causeway.

Coast Guard Headquarters, ICS Conference Room, 11:30 AM

After returning from the commandant's office, Ann had asked LaBlanc and the two non-operations-oriented members of the team to continue their respective work in other offices. LaBlanc, not sensing anything unusual in the request, opted to return to her hotel. There were things she needed to do to further her own operation.

When the three people were gone, Ann continued asking for evaluations of the morning's attacks. "Captain Briggs?"

"I agree with Fletcher and Robin: The terrorists were set to go. There's more to this than just shock value and money. My guess is that we won't hear from them again until the next attacks are set to go, and they said they'd be in touch in two days. For some reason, they seem to be on a schedule."

Ken James concurred with the others.

"That makes it unanimous," said Ann. "Doug, I want you and Fletcher to come up with attack scenarios for the remaining large ports and ways to counter those scenarios.

"We need to maintain a highly-visible presence in all ports, and I want more, but less-visible assets concentrated in the areas you determine are the most likely targets. Also, I'll ask the President to change the use-of-force rules so that our people have a better chance of surviving.

"Any questions?"

There were none. "Okay, let's get moving. We'll meet again at four o'clock unless there are any more developments. I'll let the others know."

Mark pulled Robin and Doug to one side as they were leaving the conference room.

"I'd like to talk with you both privately, if you have a few minutes," he said in a low voice.

"Whatever you have to say, Lieutenant, should be run by Admiral Gallaher first," replied Doug.

But Robin voiced her disagreement. "I think we should hear what's on his mind before deciding if the admiral needs to know. Mark, meet us in my office in ten minutes."

21

Candler's Office, Coast Guard Headquarters, 12:30 PM, Eastern Time

Mark showed up right on time and Amy Forrest, carrying her laptop computer, was with him.

Still a little thrown by being overridden by Robin, Doug launched into Mark. "Alright, Fletcher, we agreed to talk with you off the record, but not you and Forrest. Admiral Gallaher is disturbed by your involvement in this situation already, and the fact that Lieutenant Forrest was brought in at your suggestion will only exacerbate an already bad situation if she finds out about this meeting."

Mark countered, "Captain, I don't give a rat's can what Admiral Gallaher thinks about me. Or, at this point, what you think about me. We're up to our asses in alligators and they're draining the swamp. I know LaBlanc's behind this. I don't know why yet, but at least Amy and I are taking the concept seriously."

"I'm beginning to agree with Admiral Gallaher that you're being paranoid," Doug retorted. "How'd you persuade Lieutenant Forrest to help in this nonsense? I thought she had better judgment than that."

"I resent that, Captain. He didn't persuade me, I offered," snapped Amy. "And I seem to have better judgment than a number of my superior officers are exhibiting in this crisis."

"Alright, everyone, let's cool down," said Robin. "This isn't getting us anywhere. Mark, what did you want to see us about?"

"Amy's investigating Seiako's operations, and I've started looking into the companies that manage port operations both in the US and overseas. We don't have much info yet, but I'm betting we'll find a connection. The one promising lead we have is that the port facility being built in Mexico is due to begin operations within the next week. If one company or person controlled the place, they'd make billions of dollars if the US ports were shut down."

Doug was incredulous. "You're saying LaBlanc arranged to have hundreds of people murdered, millions of dollars of shipping destroyed, and created chaos in the economy for her own economic gains?"

"That's exactly what I'm saying."

"Now I know you're paranoid." Doug looked at Amy. "And you believe him?"

With a look of defiance, Amy replied: "I do, and I think you should too. What's he's saying isn't any more insane than some terrorist we've never heard about blowing up ships. From the intelligence reports I've read, there was no indication of unusual activity. Someone knows the systems and how to avoid being caught. If it originated in the Middle East or Central Asia, we would have at least picked up rumors. Even going back six months, there's nothing—no phone intercepts, e-mails, postings on web sites, large bank transfers, nothing. These people are good—they're better than anyone we've encountered since 9/11."

Mark took over the argument. "They're not making any tactical mistakes, either. The two attacks were completely different. They were well thought out and executed. As we saw in Los Angeles, the team wasn't deterred by having to kill two security people. And, as far as we know, the Norfolk attacked only used suicide teams. Let's face it, despite the self-aggrandizing verbosity of the leader, we're up against real professionals, backed by good security and logistics."

Robin asked: "Okay, Mark, if this is true, how do we beat them?"

"By thinking outside the box."

"Great, Fletcher. You're asked for solutions and you give us a cliché," Doug interjected.

Amy growled, "For god's sake, let him finish."

Openly attacked by two subordinates and not backed by Robin, Doug realized it was time to back off and open his mind. "I apologize to you both. Mark, what do you and Amy suggest? I'm really listening."

Half an hour later, Mark and Amy left to grab a late lunch. Doug went with them to pick up something for himself and Robin

As soon as she was alone, Robin asked two of her most trusted assistants, Gabe Burnbaum and Michelle Wong, to come to her office.

"As you know, the attacks this morning came only minutes after we turned down their demands, and the four attacks have closed six of the twelve major U.S. ports. Highland opposed Admiral Gallaher's appointment to head the ICS, and now he's publicly called for her resignation. In addition, he forced an outside consultant on the ICS team."

Michelle asked: "What do you want us to do?"

"I want you to find out all you can about Secretary Highland, including financial status, family background, previous assignments, friends, business and political associates, as well as anything else you can think of we should know."

"That's a lot of ground to cover," said Gabe.

"I know—and it has to be done without anyone finding out."

George Bush International Airport, Houston, Texas

The approaches to the airport were jammed as the limousine driver worked his way to the Continental Airlines terminal. Finally reaching the curb, he got out and hurried to the right side, arriving at the door just as the first of his seven passengers stepped out.

"Nice work," said the tallest of the group, handing the driver a folded hundred-dollar bill. "We appreciate you getting us here on time."

Smiling, the driver assisted the four men and three women as they pulled their carry-on luggage from the limo's trunk. Once the limo pulled away, the team split up, the three couples and Vreeland taking the airport shuttle to four different airlines. At each one, their first-class tickets, purchased weeks earlier, combined with flawless documents verifying their new identities assured priority treatment.

Los Angeles, California

Showered, fed, and somewhat rested after the attack, Lokesh's team headed for their next target. Unlike Vreeland's group, the West Coast team was driving, not flying. But, like Vreeland's team, the couples traveled separately, partly for security reasons, partly to insure that if something happened to one group, the mission wouldn't have to be aborted. And traveling in pairs would arouse less suspicion if they were stopped by a law-enforcement officer.

22

Coast Guard Headquarters, 2:45 PM, Eastern Time
Bob Davies walked into Robin's office accompanied by Amy and Doug. Robin came from behind her desk to greet him.

"Thank you for coming, Mr. Davies. I realize this must be a difficult time for you, and I'm deeply sorry about your wife," said Robin, extending her hand. She saw a man whose face was etched with grief and exhaustion, yet his shoulders where squared and his eyes held a coldness that sent a shiver down her spine.

"It's alright. I'm glad to be of help," answered the former SEAL, his eyes softening as he shook her hand. "I know your terrorist and I know why he wants Mark."

"Let's sit and you can fill me in." Once settled, she said, "Mr. Davies, Mark doesn't know you're here. I wanted a few minutes to talk with you before he came in. So tell me, how do you know the terrorist?"

"He led the ambush that night in Iraq, and Mark put a couple of forty-five slugs into him," Bob said. "Mark was too far away to see him clearly, and I didn't know until a few minutes ago that Mark hadn't told anyone in the Coast Guard about the operation.

"I was in pretty rough shape when we got back that night. This guy hit me twice in the back. My body armor stopped the bullets, but the impact damaged my spine. By the time I got out of the hospital, Mark had been sent back to the States."

Amy addressed Robin. "Now that we know where this man came from, how do we go about finding out who he is and who he might be working with?"

Before Robin could reply, there was a knock on the door and Mark entered. His first thought was: "What's this civilian doing here?" Then, "Man, he sure looks a lot like Bob Davies."

The Bob Davies clone said: "Hello, Mark. It looks like it's your beach party this time."

It took Mark only a couple of seconds to understand. "Go-Go, it's great to see you! Sorry to drag you into this mess, but we needed info."

"It's okay. I witnessed the attack in Seattle and I know who our guy is," said Bob.

"And your wife was killed in the Seattle attack. Bob, I'm so sorry." Mark moved over to Bob, who stood, and the two men hugged.

"It's okay, kid, we'll get the bastard this time," stated Bob quietly.

"What do you mean 'this time'?"

"Mark, please sit down and we'll bring you up to speed," said Robin. "Bob recognized the terrorist as the man who led the ambush in Iraq. We don't know his name yet. But I have a plan for getting that information. Bob, I want you to get in touch with your SPEC Warfare contacts. Give them all the info you can about the ambush in Iraq and see if they have anything on this guy."

"Why not go through normal channels for the info?" asked Bob.

"We believe someone on the ICS staff may be leaking info to the terrorists."

"What do you what me to do?"

Admiral Gallaher walked in unannounced and overheard Bob's question. Taking in the scene, she resolved to deal with her team's withholding of information later.

"I'll answer that," she said. "I want you to work with Captain Briggs on developing attack scenarios that the terrorists might use. Then come up with ways to block them."

Aye, aye, Admiral," said Bob reflexively. "Are we going to have anybody helping us who knows what they're doing?"

"We've pulled together the best the Coast Guard has in this area; you'll be working with them."

Forcing a smile, Bob replied, "Thank you, Admiral, but these people missed the first two times out. Is there anyone else we can call on?"

Ann answered stiffly: "Yes, your team members from Iraq will be here in the morning."

This time, Bob's smile came naturally and included his eyes. "Admiral, that'll be just fine."

Ann asked, "Captain Briggs, what have you come up with for next possible target ports?"

"The major ones are Charleston, South Carolina, the New York/New Jersey complexes, San Diego, New Orleans, and San Francisco/Oakland."

"What about Miami? Or maybe the Saint Lawrence Seaway leading to the Great Lakes?" asked Mark.

"Good question. If they hit a cruise ship in Miami or a large freighter in the Saint Lawrence, it would draw a lot of attention, but wouldn't cause a ripple economically."

"Very well," she said in a cool voice. "We'll continue this discussion at the next ICS meeting with the full team present. I suggest each of you concentrate on your individual assignments until then."

She left the office.

"What's going on with her? " Bob asked Mark.

"She thinks I'm paranoid, and that part of this is my fault."

Bob smiled and shook his head. "I see you haven't lost your talent for upsetting your superior officers."

"There's more to it than that," Robin said and briefed Bob on the situation.

"Okay, I'll keep my mouth shut about knowing the terrorist for right now. When the rest of the team gets here tomorrow, maybe we can expand our operations."

Mark thought this over for minute. "Listen, since we don't trust LaBlanc, let's mention you do know the terrorist and watch her reaction. Also the info might force her to do something she hadn't planned on. Anything to shake up the terrorists or LaBlanc will work to our benefit."

"The correct thing to do in this situation is to inform Admiral Gallaher of everything we uncover," Doug said. "However, I think we're better off by not telling her everything for the time being. When we're ready, we'll give her select material and see where it turns up. Let's see what we can do to save us all from disaster."

23

ICS Conference Room Coast Guard Headquarters, 4:00 PM, Eastern Time

Ann Gallaher introduced Bob Davies as a witness to the attack in Seattle. Then, for the first time, she told the team about Davies leading a SEAL team operation in Iraq and Fletcher's part in that operation. She finished by informing the team: "Mr. Davies identified the terrorist as the same man who led the ambush in Iraq."

Doug and Robin both saw LaBlanc's face go pale. But, quickly recovering from the apparent shock, LaBlanc cleared her throat and asked: "Do you have a name to go with the face yet?"

"Not yet," Robin answered for Ann. "However, with this latest info, we can narrow our search to former members if the Iraqi Special Security forces that disappeared after the invasion. Another factor which will help is that we're looking for someone who had access to weapons-smuggling operations."

Lieutenant Commander Jonathan Romanski wanted to know how they had determined that fact.

Doug fielded the question. "Preliminary indications are that Maindeka limpet mines made in India were used in this morning's attacks. A number of those were sold to Iraq and never accounted for after the invasion. Based on this information, and the fact that Davies's SEAL team was ambushed by someone posing as an Iraqi informant, Ms. Candler's evaluation makes a lot of sense."

"This is very interesting," responded LaBlanc. "There was a report from one of Seiako's middle-eastern representatives several years ago that dovetails with this new information. I don't remember any names being mentioned, but I'll check the report and my other sources."

"Bingo, she took the bait," thought Robin, keeping her face neutral.

"Thank you, Ms. LaBlanc," Ann Gallaher said, pleased there might finally be a break in the crisis. "I'm sure that will be extremely helpful."

The meeting lasted another two hours, encompassing reports from the team members, LANT and PAC Area commanders, and a conference call to the Whitehouse Chief of Staff, FBI, CIA, and NSA, as well as representatives from the Pentagon.

Los Angeles, CA, 4:00 PM (7:00 Eastern Time)

Los Angeles Port Police Sergeant Miguel Chaves hauled his compact body onto the patrol boat's dive platform and peeled off his dive mask. As Chaves cleared the platform, his dive partner was right behind him. A mile away the *Nordic Star* listed drunkenly across the channel, surrounded by a necklace of containers. At random intervals, one of the containers would explode, punctuating the impact of the morning's disaster as well as effectively deterring any potential salvage operations.

"We found the security guards at the base of the pier. From what I could see, each one had been stabbed through his lower jaw," he reported to Lieutenant Marie DeSalvo, assistant chief in charge of the Patrol Unit, awaiting him on the pier.

DeSalvo wasn't surprised by the report. Terrorist who blew up ships wouldn't hesitate to kill anyone that got in their way.

"We found indications that several good-sized packages had been secured to the pier about twenty feet down. As a guess, I'd say they'd been there about three weeks. We also found dive masks, fins, and six rebreather units."

Shocked, DeSalvo considered the information carefully. It meant the operation had been planned long before, and the enhanced security by Port Police and Coast Guard hadn't made any difference. It was not a pleasant conclusion.

"Good work, Sergeant. I'll notify the chief. Let's get the dive gear to the lab as soon as possible, then we'll recover the bodies."

La Petite Femme Bistro, Georgetown

LaBlanc and Golden didn't talk on the ride from Coast Guard headquarters. However, once seated in the restaurant, LaBlanc quietly exploded. "Al-Hishma lied to you when he said no one could identify him. The SEAL team leader can, they were face to face at the ambush. That stupid, arrogant idiot could cost us the whole operation."

"I thought al-Hishma killed the SEAL team leader who saw him and Fletcher was the only other one who got a look at al-Hishma. That's what every piece of intelligence we were able to find showed," Gwen countered.

"Well, the information was wrong, and they're trying to track down al-Hishma's activities and contacts," snapped LaBlanc.

"There's nothing linking you to him and the attacks."

"We'll see. At the meeting, I sensed Gallaher and Candler were holding back information. Call Highland and tell him to find out exactly what Gallaher knows and what other information they're looking for. I need to know now. What's the good of owning a Cabinet secretary if he can't come up with classified information?"

Gwen Goldin, less upset at the news, asked: "What are you going to do?"

"I'm going to give them his name to start with. I'm not sure it'll do them much good, but it'll buy me more credibility with Gallaher. Also, we'll have Highland let the media know that it was his person, not Gallaher's, that provided the information. Since Story didn't fire Gallaher before, this may do the trick."

As LaBlanc vented, Goldin poured a couple of glasses of wine, and, when her boss had wound down, handed her one.

"Okay, you've given me some bad news, now I've got good news for you." Goldin smiled. "Our Mexican port started full operations today, and the first container ships diverted from Los Angeles will arrive in two days. Because of the turmoil, and a little help from our holding companies, fees and other costs have increased significantly.

"As we anticipated, Terra Marine, PSA and Dubai Ports World are losing significant amounts of money. I estimate by early next week, we'll be able to buy what's left of Terra cheaply, and begin to force the other two out. Even if Gallaher and company get lucky, we still achieve what we set out to do."

LaBlanc had come to the same conclusions, but wanted to see if Goldin was thinking along similar lines.

"I'm going to let Demivov know about Davies and al-Hishma. I don't want him compromised, and this should give him enough time to cover his tracks. Also, if Fletcher proves smarter than he looks, I want a team in place to take care of him."

24

WEDNESDAY

Coast Guard Headquarters, 8:00 AM, Eastern Time

After three days cooped up in a sunless cubicle, Mark was going stir crazy. Although he had moved out of a small, secondrate hotel into a suite at the Doubletree, it still wasn't home. Even his morning runs and noon walks didn't relieve the stress. Admiral Gallaher was keeping him at arm's length, not letting him be part of the ICS team. And none of his digging into to a LaBlanc-Highland connection had turned up anything.

Mark got up to stretch, glancing at Amy sitting across from him as he did. Bright, beautiful, and gutsy, he'd trust her with his life. The problem was he wasn't sure she'd give him the time of day. And any relationship would be complicated since she was black and he was white. He didn't care, but did she?

Amy looked up and caught Mark gazing at her. She gave him a vague friendly smile, and looked back down at her computer screen to hide her feelings. He wasn't at all like her first impression of him as Mr. Macho. Working with him over the past couple of days, she sensed a lot of warmth and caring underneath that exterior. But he was white and might not be interested in her. And, anyway, it wasn't the right time to explore any personal relationship with anyone—white or black.

"I hope we get something soon from the Intel people Robin had us contact," she said to break the silence.

"Yeah, me too," replied Mark. "If we can nail this guy's background, maybe we can see what he's been up to recently."

"I'll hold down the fort if you want to take a break. There's no point in both of us being stuck here."

"Great. I think I'll head down to Captain Briggs's office to see what he and Bob have come up with. I'll take my computer and log in there. Hopefully we'll have something before the ten o'clock ICS meeting."

Before heading out the door, Mark asked: "I hope I'm not being out of line, but when this is over, would you have dinner with me?"

Unable to prevent a smile, Amy looked up at Mark. "I'd like that."

Coast Guard Headquarters, 8:15 AM, Eastern Time

Mark heard shouting as he approached Doug's office. Breaking into a run, he skidded around the corner and ran smack into the back of a large man standing in Doug's doorway. The man he'd run into spun around, pinning Mark against the door frame.

"Hey, Gator, we've got to stop meeting like this," Mark said, recognizing the face at the other end of the arm. He smiled and wrapped his other arm around Mark in a hug that Mark returned.

The two entered Doug's office where Mark was greeted by a hail of insults from the rest of the old SEAL team, insults he returned with enthusiasm. Once things had quieted down, Doug spoke up, "Nice to see you, Mark, but what are you doing here?"

"We haven't heard anything from overseas, so I thought I'd come over here and see what's going on. And I've come up with some off-the-wall attack scenarios I wanted to discuss with you. If I'd known the SEALs had landed, I'd have stayed with Amy."

Gator asked: "Amy? Who's Amy?".

Bob's response, "Later, Gator," brought groans from everybody.

Mark noticed Spencer, Grim, and Patton were missing. He knew enough not to ask where they were or if they were still alive.

Trying to regain control of the situation, Doug said, "Okay, Mark, get set up and we'll bring you up to speed. First, let's start with the introductions. On your right is Admiral Ken James, DOG CO; Commander William Oberlander, who's in charge of the Marine Safety and Security Teams, and next to him is Master Chief Petty Officer Peter Hillabrant, the Master Chief of the Teams. Next is Captain Debra Williams, Port Safety Units' CO. The Marine is Colonel Miguel Sanchez from Quantico; he's in charge of the DOG unit training down there on the Marine side. You know the rest of this motley crew.

"For those of you who don't know him, this is Lieutenant Mark Fletcher, the only man the terrorist will talk to—and, thanks to Bob, we believe we now know why."

"What was all the commotion I heard before?" asked Mark.

Colonel Sanchez answered, "The SEALs had just arrived and were getting reacquainted."

Suppressing a smile, Mark said: "It's something I've seen before—must have been real ugly."

"Here's what we've got so far," said Captain Smith, picking up the conversation. "Suicide attacks with explosive-laden boats and automatic weapons fired from those boats during the first attacks. The second attacks used hull-mounted charges we believe were placed by swimmers, who, later, when the charges detonated, fired on the rescue boats."

All of them had seen the news coverage of the attack on the cruiser, and Bob filled them in on what he'd seen. No one commented on the first attacks; they realized the terrorists employed tactics tailored to the Navy and Coast Guard's weaknesses.

Captain Smith continued, "During the second attack, we lost a number of people because the machine guns on the patrol boats couldn't be elevated enough to fire back, and the mounts were unshielded."

Web asked Captain Oberlander and Master Chief Petty Officer Hillabrant, "How'd the swimmers get close enough to plant the charges with concussion grenades going off in the water around them? What about gun shields?"

Both men, as well as Lieutenant Colonel Sanchez, flushed at the question.

"Yeah," Bob piped up as the silence stretched out, "those are good questions. What're the answers?"

Finally Captain Oberlander said, "We don't use concussion grenades. With the anti-swimmer system we thought there'd be no need for them. We also didn't think splinter shields on the gun mounts were needed."

"You've got to be shitting me!" exploded Sandman. "What else didn't you think there'd be a need for? You stupid bastards, you got people killed for no reason."

"Back off," Oberlander said to Sandman.

"I won't back off. You're a bunch of amateurs playing at being big, bad, Special Forces types. You don't have a clue."

"Sandman's right," snapped Mark. "I know the Port Security Units have been to Iraq, but none of your MSST or the Maritime Security Response teams have combat experience. I've always believed they were a waste of assets—and the last attacks proved I was right."

Fighting to control of his temper, Doug intervened. "Ease off, Fletcher, we'll address the issue later. Let's get back to examining the weak points of the potential target harbors and what you've come up with."

Sanchez, who hadn't said anything during the exchange, caught the look Oberlander shot at Mark and knew Mark had just made an enemy.

When everyone had settled down, Doug brought them up to speed on the report from Los Angeles. As everyone absorbed the impact of the findings, Doug asked Mark to explain what he'd come up with. Mark began by reviewing the tactics used in the four attacks, concentrating on the differences rather than the similarities.

"The first two were costly in casualties, and were geared toward gaining massive media coverage in addition to shutting down two of the eight choke points. If Bob hadn't seen the Seattle team leaving, we'd think both attacks were done by suicide squads.

"The second two attacks used professionals to set limpet mines, booby-trap containers, and work in unison to kill our people and disrupt rescue operations. Knowing the leader was part of Iraqi Intelligence indicates—to me anyway—an individual with the knowledge and contacts to successfully accomplish what he's trying to do.

"Captain Briggs's info that the limpets had been prepositioned reinforces my conclusion that however the next attacks are to be executed, everything is already in place."

"Brilliant deductions, Lieutenant," Oberlander sneered. "How do you propose to stop them?"

"Begin by thinking like a terrorist."

Master Chief Petty Officer Hillabrant smirked. "That should be easy for you since you're part of the reason we're in this mess. You've been nothing but trouble since you were a Boot Seaman."

Smiling, Mark replied quietly: "Careful, Master Chief. The last time we had a go-round it was two days before you could get out of bed, and a month before you could eat solid food."

Ignoring Hillabrant's reddening face and the SEALs' laughter, Mark walked to the map pinned to one wall. Circled in yellow were the eight access points Doug was concerned about, and four also had a red "X" through them.

"I don't believe the terrorists will repeat themselves. My guess is that they'll use naval mines and we won't see even one member of the teams."

This time it was Admiral James who questioned Mark's conclusions. Captain Debra Williams listened as the discussion ranged back and forth before she interjected, "Do any of you know about the Italian mines found on board ships tied up in Umm Qasr? While I was with PSU 918 we found literally barrels full on them."

Bob Davies admired how deftly Williams shifted the discussion over to Mark's side and ensured anything else she had to say would be taken seriously by everyone in the room.

Oberlander answered, "I read that they're among the most difficult to detect. So you think Fletcher might be correct?"

Williams nodded. "Yes, I reached the same conclusions he did. Fletcher's not the only one who thinks like a terrorist. Our time would be better spent trying to counter this than debating whether or not Fletcher's right. We've got less than twenty-four hours."

"I'm going to cut this discussion short and make a command decision to go with the mine-attack scenario," Doug said. "The first thing is to determine the most likely targets."

The parameters were limited to the number of choke points left and had to take into consideration that in the first two attacks the terrorists hit one of the points on each coast simultaneously. The remaining targets on the West Coast were Long Beach, San Diego and San Francisco. There were more on the East and Gulf Coasts: New York/Newark, Charleston, the Mississippi below New Orleans, and Port Arthur, Texas.

Admiral James brought up the point that no one present was an expert on naval mines or what the Navy's current counter-mine capabilities were. While the team narrowed down the list of potential target ports, Doug took Mark with him to see Ann Gallaher. They needed her okay to get in touch with the Navy Mine Warfare and Explosive Ordnance Detachment commands.

25

Coast Guard Headquarters, 9:00 AM, Eastern Time

Seated in Ann's office ten minutes later, Doug explained what they'd come up with regarding the next attacks. Though doubtful about their conclusions, she called Admiral George Nathan, Chief of Naval Operations (CNO).

"I think you're on the money with this," the CNO replied. "Hold on while I round up the people we'll need."

When he came back on line, Nathan started with introductions. "I have Rear Admirals Joe Fitzgerald, CO Naval Mine and ASW in Corpus Christi; Ed Cronan, CO of the Naval Mine and ASW in San Diego; and Mr. Lee Hunt, former Director, Naval Studies Board of the National Academy of Sciences National Research Council, and now a Naval Warfare consultant. Lee's mine warfare experience goes back to clearing mines and obstacles from the Okinawa invasion beaches with gunfire during World War II, and sweeping the mines in the inland waters of Japan during the Occupation. Lee, will you get us started?"

Lee began: "Gladly. The way I see it, if the terrorists have already planted their mines, and we have only twenty-four hours, we're facing an almost impossible situation. If we're lucky, we can do it. If we're not lucky, we may have already suffered our first ship casualty."

The stillness on the line was finally broken by the CNO, who cleared his throat, and said, "You said almost impossible. Does that mean we have at least a slim chance of beating this thing?"

"Yes, sir, there is a slim chance, but it's not going to be pretty, and it's going to require instantaneous command decisions from each of you."

"Okay, Lee, shoot."

"Gentlemen, a mine doesn't sink ships that don't move. Admiral Gallaher, I recommend you send out an order stopping the sailing of every ship displacing ten thousand tons or greater in each of the potential target ports."

Anticipating the next question, Hunt added, "Stopping all large ship traffic is exactly what the terrorists hope to do. Our job now is to find and remove the mines in a time much shorter than it would take us to remove sunken ships."

Ann Gallaher said: "Doug, call Admiral Story and ask him to get that order out, freezing all ships, ten thousand tons or greater, in place, until further notice. That will cover any bulk carriers, container ships, and tankers. You know which ports."

"Admiral, may I suggest that the order not go into effect until midnight, and that no one outside this group be notified of the order until an hour before it goes into effect?" Mark said. "I know it's a risk, but we don't want the information of what we're doing leaked to the terrorists. If it is, they might have time to react to our counter-measures and trigger the mines early."

It was a reasonable request even with the risks it entailed.

"Okay, Lieutenant, we'll do as you suggest."

Hearing Ann's order, Hunt said: "Thanks, Admiral. We've just bought ourselves a little wiggle room, but not much, and we're in poor shape to make use of it."

Admiral Nathan asked the question uppermost in everyone's mind: "Lee, what's your evaluation of what we're facing?"

"There are a number of suitable mines available on the open market, notably those from Italy and Sweden, but there are two reasons I don't think the terrorists will choose them.

They're computer-controlled, which means the terrorists have to be quite thoroughly trained to properly operate them, and buying them in small numbers by a non-state customer is too obvious.

"The Russians, however, have provided their older, and simpler to operate, mines to at least ten, perhaps eleven countries. I'm betting that the terrorists got their mines from North Korea, Iran or Cuba, and the MDM-1 mine is a good choice. The MDM-1 is a magnetic/acoustic bottom mine with a 2000-pound charge." He paused for a moment. " If the terrorists can figure out how to disconnect the acoustic sensor, I think they'll do it because of the high acoustic background in crowded ports. But we can't afford to count on that possibility.

"Ordinarily we'd only do mine-hunting in situations like this, with the disarming of the mines handled by Navy EOD (Explosive Ordinance Disposal) personnel to avoid the collateral damage that might occur from a mine detonation. We can't afford the time to do that now, so sweeping with mine detonation is the only option."

Hunt sensed he was taking too long and picked up his pace. "We have twelve MH-53E Sea Dragon helicopters at Norfolk. I recommend we spread those twelve through the five priority ports. Tell them they'll need their MK-104 acoustic sweep and MK-105 magnetic sweep only. You may want to consider using C-5 aircraft to get them to the more distant locations to save time and engine wear. And, remember, there'll be areas where the helicopters can't sweep because of bridges and overhead wires."

Addressing Admiral Cronan, Hunt said, "Admiral, EOD-7 in San Diego has the MHS-1, the twenty-four ton SWATH. She's already done a survey of San Diego Bay. I recommend you order her to immediately begin a change detection survey. If there's something new on the bottom, she'll turn it up.

"She has two sister craft in Seattle. I recommend you send them by C-5 to New Orleans. You'll have to have her trucked from the airport. Tell them to begin taking the cabin off so she'll fit in the C-5."

Hunt saw confusion on a few faces and quickly explained: "The MHS SWATH—an acronym for small water-plane area twin hull—is forty feet long by eighteen feet wide, weighing approximately twenty-four tons. The mine-hunting version can be deployed to any region of the world via a fifteen-ton marine truck, C-5 Galaxy heavy-duty transport aircraft or ship. It takes only 240 bolts to remove the crew compartment from the hull. The entire unit can be set to load on a C-5 in three hours."

Nathan picked up that lead. "While Lee was talking, I arranged for two C-5s to be ready to go in Seattle by the time the SWATHs are palletized. It'll take them about five hours from there to New Orleans, so we'll be able to begin operations about twelve hours from now."

"I'll have EOD Mobile Unit Six out of Charleston and EOD Mobile Unit Two from Norfolk on scene when the SWATHs arrive," contributed Joe Fitzgerald.

After a short pause, Ann asked: "Is that it?"

Hunt replied: "I'm afraid not. Now is when we get down and dirty. Admiral Nathan, ask your aide to find out who manufactures bar magnets. And Admiral Fitzgerald, ask your aide to contact the Naval Coastal Systems Center at Panama City and ask what size bar magnets we need to sweep a magnetic mine with a coarse setting. Then order one hundred of them—twenty of them to be shipped fastest to the five ports.

"And, while he's on the horn to Panama City, find out if there's an old chief there who still knows how to build rattle bars. Tell him to begin turning them out as fast as the shop can manage, and begin similar distribution."

Hunt wasn't done yet. "Admiral Gallaher, please have your small cutters in each port to stand by to begin towing the combination of the two. We'll need ten tows in each port, and if you don't have enough, press into service any craft with enough horsepower to tow at twenty knots. In the 1980s, we had a Craft of Opportunity Program designed to use civilian craft for handling mine counter-measures gear. It's time we put it back in service. I'm betting these COOP craft will be the ones to detonate the mines."

Hunt sat back in his seat with a sigh. "That's the best we can do. The rest is left to luck and the hard work of those in the field."

26

Coast Guard Headquarters, 9:30 AM, Eastern Time
Amy Forrest walked into Robin's office, closed the door behind her and sat down.

"And to what do I owe the honor of this unexpected visit?" Robin asked with a smile. Sliding a folder across to Robin, Amy said: "Evelyn LaBlanc and Seiako."

Arching her eyebrows in a question, Robin picked up the folder and began reading its contents. Ten minutes later, Robin put the folder down. "This is a good. How soon will you be able to nail down the specifics?"

"I'll have the rest by this afternoon."

"Sounds good to me," said Robin.

After Amy left Robin called Gabe Burnbaum and Michelle Wong to see what they had found out about Highland.

Galveston, Texas
Following up on the Los Angeles Port Police report, Galveston Police Department divers located six sets of dive gear. While the divers were searching, members of the ICS called all the dive shops for information on recent sales of rebreather units. Three shops had sold the units as part of complete scuba-gear packages between three and six weeks ago. None of the salespeople noticed anything unusual about buyers and couldn't give accurate descriptions. The only memorable thing about the transactions was that the people paid cash.

While the divers searched the piers, Coast Guard units, working with Navy EOD teams, cleared the dozens of containers which had fallen from *Evangeline*'s decks. A team from TITAN Salvage had flown in the night before and was surveying the ship. Another TITAN team was in Los Angeles engaged in the same process.

McCormick & Schmick's, Washington, D.C., 12:30 PM, Eastern Time

The change from bright, noisy street to McCormick & Schmick's subdued lighting and dark wood interior was soothing. After giving her name, LaBlanc followed the hostess to the table where Gwen was studying the luncheon menu selections. She had been there long enough to order a bottle of wine and some appetizers she knew her boss liked.

LaBlanc was pensive as she slid into the booth. Seeing her look, Gwen asked: "What's the matter?"

LaBlanc filled Gwen in on the morning's ICS meeting, and that, as planned, she'd given al-Hishma's name to the team members, unaware Robin had already come up with it. She continued, "Fletcher and his crew are digging deeper than I thought they would."

As LaBlanc poured herself a glass of wine, Gwen asked, "How are they doing it? How do you know?"

"I overheard part of a conversation about Forrest looking into the operations of Seiako and its competitors. She doesn't have all the details of what we've been doing, but she's getting close. It concerns me that they were able to do this without word getting back to me."

"What have they found so far?"

"Only that Seiako's been expanding their operations in a number of ports, and that Terra Marine has been unsuccessful in attempts to widen operations in others. Also, Terra Marine has suffered a number of costly accidents over the past three years, and has been hit with strikes against their facilities."

"So they haven't caught on that you're behind this, or that Terra Marine is near bankruptcy. And, so far, there's no word that they know about how much we own of the Mexican operation?"

Evelyn took another sip of wine. "That's right. Nonetheless, I think given enough time, she'll find out."

"Look on the bright side of all this. Shipping rates are skyrocketing; we're doing well with our Wall Street ventures; and the Pentagon is looking into supply sources from Europe, the majority of which we control. And, in three days, it won't matter what she finds out. It'll be too late to do anything."

"I know, but I don't like loose ends. And we still need to make Highland more visible."

"How do you propose to do that?"

With a sly smile, Evelyn told her.

27

Coast Guard Headquarters, 2:00 PM, Eastern Time

Robin, Amy, Doug, and Mark almost collided outside of Ann Gallaher's office suite. "Why this sudden meeting request and why here?" Doug asked.

Robin replied: "We've found out what's behind the attacks." After a brief discussion with Gallaher's aide, they were shown into Ann's office. Annoyed at the interruption, Ann asked curtly why they were there.

"I've found out the reason behind the attacks, and it's more than just a terrorist seeking retribution. But I'll begin with that," Robin answered. "Colonel Quhir Nabi-Ulmalhamsh al-Hishma, formerly of the Iraqi Intelligence Special Security, was last seen on March eighteenth, 2003. After the invasion, no one's sure if he was killed or decided to disappear. Another piece of useful information was that his last meeting was with Colonel Pytor Ivanov Demivov, GRU, Russian Army Intelligence. Further investigation turned up info that Demivov has ties to Russian organized crime."

"That's all well and good," Ann interjected impatiently, "but it still sounds like extortion wrapped around a personal vendetta."

"That's just the tip of the iceberg," replied Robin. "Several of us thought Highland's insistence that LaBlanc come on as a consultant was strange. Lieutenant Forrest began looking into LaBlanc and Seiako while Lieutenant Fletcher concentrated on companies running port operations. Concurrently, I had Highland checked out." Knowing Gallaher's dislike for Mark, Robin decided to take the responsibility for Amy's digging into Seiako at Mark's request.

On the verge of losing her temper, Ann interrupted: "Why wasn't I informed of these investigations? Ms. Candler, you have grossly overstepped your authority."

Ignoring the Admiral's displeasure, Robin continued. "We know LaBlanc owns Seiako. Fletcher is fairly sure LaBlanc's behind the attacks, but wasn't sure what she stood to gain. Amy locked down the info. Using contacts in Europe, she was able to locate several holding companies

Amy then explained about the new Mexican port, and that by using holding companies as a blind, LaBlanc personally controlled most of the operation.

"That may be unethical, but it's not illegal," Ann coolly responded.

Robin continued. "LaBlanc is a heavy contributor to Highland's political campaigns. We've also uncovered several off-shore accounts he maintains that don't show up on his taxes."

Ann started to interrupt again, but Robin didn't give her the chance.

"Highland was assigned to Kosovo several years ago at the same time Demivov was there. Shortly after Highland returned, his political career went into high gear, his off-shore accounts began to grow steadily, and LaBlanc started backing him.

"We know Demivov, through his crime connections, is involved in the sex-slave trade. We also know while stationed in Iraq he was involved with al-Hishma and smuggling operations. Both of which require access to shipping, and a number of the shipping transactions were through freight forwarders fronting for Seiako."

Gallaher still looked angry, but she was listening.

"Here's where it all comes together. Demivov knows al-Hishma and has ties to LaBlanc through Seiako; Highland has ties to Demivov and LaBlanc; and LaBlanc controls the only major port facility capable of competing with US ports. If the majority of our ports are closed, she makes millions of dollars. If Highland comes off as the hero who thwarts the terrorists, his political career skyrockets. With a presidential election next year, he's in a good position to win.

Stunned by the news, Ann didn't say anything for several minutes, thinking it was too fantastic, too monstrous to be true. Why would anyone murder hundreds of people, destroy millions of dollars worth of ships, and cause untold economic hardship just for personal gain? It had been done before by nations, but not by the efforts of one person.

As she was beginning to form her response to these wild accusations, the phone rang. Glancing at it, the Caller ID showed the name STEVEN HIGHLAND. Nonplussed, Ann put the call on speaker.

"Good afternoon Mr. Secretary."

"Good afternoon, Admiral. Do you have a few minutes to chat?"

Confused by the friendly tone, Ann answered: "Of course. What's on your mind?"

"Ann, if I may call you Ann, I feel we've been at loggerheads for too long, and I'd like to change that if it's not too late. We got off to a bad start in the current crisis, and I'd like to find out what I might be able to do to further your efforts."

"That's very considerate of you, Mr. Secretary. What do you have in mind?"

"I haven't had the chance to meet the people who I gather are your core staff: Captain Briggs, Ms. Candler, Lieutenant

Forrest, Mr. Davies, and, of course, Lieutenant Fletcher. Perhaps we could get together informally this evening. We could take care of introductions and then see if there's something constructive for me to do."

Doug grabbed a piece of paper. He wrote PLEASE *accept his offer!!!* on it and handed it to Ann, who read it.

"That's very generous of you, and, on behalf of myself and the others, I accept your invitation. Where and when would you like to meet?"

"How about this evening around nine o'clock? To keep this as discrete as possible, my assistant has offered to let me use her place near Rock Creek Gardens for our meeting."

Curiouser and curiouser, Mark thought, listening to the conversation.

Now thoroughly perplexed, Ann replied: "That sounds fine."

"Good, I'll have Lena send you the directions. Thanks, Ann, and I look forward to seeing you later."

The four people gathered around her desk were grinning as Ann broke the connection.

"Alright, what's so amusing?"

Doug replied: "The timing for one thing. Another is it gets all the troublemakers in one place at one time." Doug looked at Mark. "Ambush?"

"Yeah. It sure smells like one."

Ann said: "His offer makes sense to me. We need to smooth things out. You're not aware of it, but the secretary put pressure on the commandant to relieve me as head of the ICS. This sounds as close to an apology for his action as I'm likely to get."

"After trying to get you fired and possibly ruining your career, he's making nice and you trust him?" put in Robin.

Mark added: "To quote Fredrick Forsyth, 'Trust is a silly and superfluous weakness.' What did Robin just get finished telling you about Highland? This guy's in it up to his ears.

This is a perfect setup. He gets us all out in the open on a known route at a known time. I'll bet the directions lead through a perfect ambush area."

"Lieutenant, I told you before, I think you're being paranoid."

Mark slowly stood up, placed his clenched fists on Ann's desk, leaned over as close as he could get to her and said very softly: "Admiral, just because you're paranoid doesn't mean someone's not out to get you.

"Personally, I think you're full of shit, and this is further proof of it. The call was too timely. We know there's another attack scheduled for tomorrow, and a few rounds of ammunition would take out most of the senior staff. If you're killed, Highland takes over and becomes a hero. What's it going to take to convince you we're right? A nine-millimeter bullet between the eyes? It's time to either lead, follow, or get out of the way."

The soft, almost gentle way Mark delivered his attack sounded more menacing to Ann and the others than if he had shouted it.

Gently pulling Mark back from the desk, Amy said: "Easy, Mark, easy."

Mark sat down without taking his eyes off Ann. Calmly meeting his gaze, she said: "Lieutenant, the next time you speak to me like that, I'll have you court-martialled."

"I'd rather be court-martialled than be buried with full military honors."

"Shut up, Mark," Ann replied without rancor, then addressed Doug. "Captain, I'm going to indulge Lieutenant Fletcher's paranoia. Please ask Mr. Davies and his men to join us. If it's a setup, let's see how we can use their experience to our advantage."

28

Washington, D.C., 8:30 PM, Eastern Time

Leaving Coast Guard headquarters in the warm twilight evening, the ten people split up in two SUVs. Bob was in the lead with Ann driving while Web, Rico and Gator sat behind them. Doug drove the second SUV, while Robin, in the right front passenger seat, literally rode shotgun. In the back, Amy was wedged between Mark on her right and Sandman on her left.

Showing no outward concern, the SEALs regaled Ann with sea stories as they drove down through downtown DC and moved into the northwestern quadrant toward Rock Creek Park. The mood changed, however, as the small convoy exited off Military Road, NW and took two quick left turns onto Beach Drive, NW, leaving the developed areas behind to become completely surrounded by woods.

By the time they reached Rock Creek Park, Gator and Sandman had distributed SPEAR body armor, PVS-15 night-vision goggles, and Fabrique Nationale FN SCAR assault rifles to their companions. Doug, Mark, Bob, Web and Rico took SCAR-H /Mk 17s because it fires the 7.62 mm round. Robin and Amy took SCAR-L/MK 16s which fires the smaller 5.56 mm bullet.

Sandman, who liked heavier fire power, had a SCAR Light with a FN EGLM 40mm grenade launcher attached.

"Sandman, not to raise too fine a point, but what the hell are you doing carrying this stuff around?" Robin asked, amazed by the small arsenal.

"Like the American Express card, I never leave home without it. I just never know when it might come in handy."

Colonel Pytor Ivanov Demivov was not happy. He'd had only seven hours to mount the operation, which was about twenty-four hours too little. Getting the men and weapons hadn't been a problem, but he would have preferred to have a couple of RPGs. Ideally, improvised explosive devices (IEDs) would have been his method of choice, but mid-week in a high-traffic area they couldn't be relied upon, so it was back to an old-fashioned ambush.

The ambush site was perfect. He'd established the kill zone between Sherrill Drive and Wise Drive, where the ground starts to rise between fifty and a hundred yards away from the road, with a flat, grassy area about ten yards wide before the tree line. There were no street lights, and the closest houses were 600 yards away, behind the heavily wooded hills.

Unlike al-Hishma's disdain for SEALs' fighting ability and LaBlanc's condescending attitude about their intelligence, Demivov knew from experience he faced world-class warriors. Even Fletcher was dangerous. He wasn't sure about the black girl, the FBI agent or the captain, which added to his worries. The adage "professionals are predictable, it's the amateurs that are dangerous" came to mind.

His contact reported the SEALS as part of the group in the SUVs, none of the party appeared to be armed or wearing body armor when they left Coast Guard headquarters. But you just couldn't trust those damned SEALs. They might have weapons stashed in the SUVs. The report also mentioned the two primary targets, Gallaher and Davies, were sitting in the front seat of the lead SUV. Of the eight men he had, Demivov assigned two of them as snipers to take out Gallaher and Davies. Those two, at least, had to be sure kills.

Traffic control on Beach Drive was another problem. They couldn't stop it too early, but had to ensure no non-target vehicles were in the kill zone at the wrong time. Fortunately, traffic was light and no cars had gone by for the last five minutes. Lighting another Marlboro, he concluded waiting was the worst part of any operation.

As he snapped the Zippo lighter shut a call came through: "Post One calling. They're approaching Brigham Drive."

"Good, place the barricades and then close up behind them. Post Two, close the road below Sherrill Drive and position your vehicle as planned."

The waiting was over.

29

Rock Creek Park, Maryland, 9:00, Eastern Time PM

"Go-Go, we got company, a SUV about a hundred yards back," Sandman called over their radio net from the last car.

They had rounded a slight right-hand bend, and could see the road curved to their left a little ways ahead.

The bad guys picked a good spot, Bob thought. Too bad for them.

"Looks like this is it. Everybody locked and loaded?"

There were eight affirmatives. Ann didn't answer, but Bob saw her white-knuckled grip on the steering wheel.

Looking around, Bob saw the target vehicle and realized Ann was approaching a blind turn.

"Tap your brakes once and begin to ease back," he ordered Ann, and began passing on instructions to the rest of the team. "We're going to do this in the next two minutes in total darkness. Right now pop the dome lights out so there's no light when we open the doors. When I give the word, douse your headlights. Doug, as soon as you do that, turn left across the road.

Ann, when the lights go out, turn right, blocking the road. As soon as you stop moving, everybody bail out and head for the ditches along the road. Got it?"

"Roger."

"Seems like old times," Web chuckled.

"Yeah, but I'm getting too old for this shit," said Rico.

"I've always said it's not the years, it's the mileage that gets you," finished Gator.

Demivov, stationed in the woods well to one side of the kill zone, watched the two sets of approaching headlights followed by a third set about hundred meters behind. "So far, so good," he muttered.

The two closest sets of lights went out.

"What the fuck's going on?" he muttered, and called to his team: "It's a setup. Open fire."

Ann braced herself as Bob counted down: "Three, two, one. Go. Go. Go."

She killed the lights and hit the brakes. As the car slewed to a stop, Ann slapped off her seat belt, hit the door handle and bolted for the ditch. She had taken two steps when a bullet ripped into her head, sending her sprawling onto the open pavement.

On the other side, Web cleared the car before it had completely stopped and sprinted for the ditch, thinking Bob was close behind. But, just as Bob was getting ready to dive out the right side, the windshield shattered under a hail of bullets. He glanced over his shoulder in time to see Ann hit.

"Noooooo," he screamed, swinging around and plunging out the other door, the air around him filled with glass and shrapnel. Reaching Ann, Bob snatched up her limp form and carried it to the protecting ditch, a trail of blood marking their passage.

When Doug heard: "...two, one. Go. Go. Go," he spun the steering wheel, instantly throwing the car into a ninety-degree turn.

Mark said to Amy, "When we hit the ditch, stay close behind me."

"I don't need your protection."

"And I don't need an argument right now, just do it."

Her retort was cut short when Doug slammed the car to a stop. Mark followed Amy out the back door with bullets throwing up chunks of pavement around their legs. A piece of it hit Mark; he staggered into Amy, knocking her headfirst down the slope. She landed hard, on her back.

"You clumsy ape, get off of me," she gasped.

Mark, gritting his teeth against the pain, started off down the ditch, Amy following. After moving a short distance, he eased his head up over the lip of the ditch to see if he could get a shot at their attackers. Mark's head had just cleared the lip when two of the attackers on their flanks ripped loose bursts. Amy had lifted her head, mimicking Mark's movements. When the flashing gun muzzles swung towards her, she froze, her mind recalling the image of the drug-runner's bullets tearing towards her helicopter.

In the midst of his dive for cover, Mark saw Amy freeze just as a burst of automatic scythed over them. Mark grabbed her vest and pulled her behind him.

Getting into position, Sandman fired a grenade into the enemy SUV, killing the two men crouched behind it. Robin nailed one of the flankers with a three round burst and Doug took care of the second one.

Once clear of their SUV, Rico, Gator, and Web shot out the headlights of a vehicle that had blocked the road ahead of them. Sandman crawled forward to join them, followed shortly by Doug. Bob covered Ann, and did the best he could to bandage her bleeding head wound. Mark, Robin, and a badly shaken-up Amy covered the rear in case the bad guys were reinforced.

When Sandman arrived, Web asked him: "You having fun yet?"

"Yeah, lots. But we're still stuck here."

The firing had stopped momentarily. Bob joined the others and began giving orders: "Web and Gator, start working around to the left. Rico, you and Doug go right. Locate and eliminate the snipers. We'll give you a sixty-second start and then Sandman takes out the SUV ahead of us."

Demivov watched as a supposedly easy operation turned into a nightmare. In less than two minutes, half his team had been killed and the surviving four were on the defensive. From his vantage point, he'd seen Gallaher and Davies go down, as well as some of the SEALs, so that part was a success. Demivov started to order a withdrawal when the night was split apart for the second time as Sandman's grenade totaled the remaining SUV and the two men on either side of it.

"Get out, get out NOW!" Demivov called to the snipers. "They'll be coming for you."

One responded "Da," followed shortly by a Cajun-accented voice saying: "Sorry, sir, I don't think this one's going to be able to."

Without another word, Demivov, as quietly as possible, headed for his car and safety.

After the firestorm had passed, the silence was strange. No one moved for several minutes. Doug's shout "All clear forward," quickly followed by Marks's "All clear aft," brought relief to everyone.

Bob, getting the first-aid kit and flashlight from the lead SUV, began examining Ann's wound. A bullet had opened a gash across the top of her head. Although bloody, it didn't look too bad.

Doug called Robin over and said: "We need this area sealed off immediately. Get a hold of your friends and get them here ASAP. None of this can make the news." Hearing sirens approaching, he paused for a moment. "I think Mark and I can hold the locals, or at least the lower echelon ones, for a while."

With the calls "All clear forward" and "All clear aft," Amy pried Mark's grip loose without looking at him. Freed, she stepped back.

Softly he asked: "What happened to you back there?"

"The go-fast," she replied as explanation.

Mark nodded and touched her shoulder. Amy flinched at his touch and Mark dropped his hand away.

"I'm sorry," he said.

A tear rolled down Amy's cheek. "It's not you, Mark," she said huskily and wrapped her arms around him in a fierce hug, her body shaking.

Mark held her as tightly as she held him. "It's okay, it's okay."

Gator, Rico and Sandman came over.

"He's right, Amy, we've all been through it," Rico reassured her.

Gator knew something was needed to break the tension, so he yelled, "Hey, Web."

"Yeah, Gator, what ya want?"

"I'm gettin' too old for this shit."

"Well, Gator," his friend called back, "it's not the years, it's the mileage."

30

THURSDAY

Georgetown, D. C., 2:30 AM Eastern Time

After Robin's FBI friends cleaned-up the scene, and Ann's wound and a plethora of cuts and abrasions on the others had been tended to, the group went to Robin and Doug's apartment.

"Sure as hell somebody broke the faith," was Gator's first comment after they were gathered in the living room.

No one disagreed, and they dispassionately discussed who could have betrayed them. It came down to Highland, but it was decided he didn't have the guts or resources to pull off an ambush.

"So who else? LaBlanc?" asked Amy.

I'm convinced it had to be LaBlanc." confirmed Ann. Mark said: "We need to protect ourselves from another attack. Any ideas?"

"Yeah, let's play dead," suggested Rico. "They'll believe some of us were killed, so let them keep believing it."

Doug nodded. "I like that idea, and it'll be another way of smoking out Highland and LaBlanc."

"Who's going to be dead?" asked Sandman.

"I suggest it be Admiral Gallaher, Bob, and maybe Rico and Web," proposed Amy.

Mark added, "That's good, and how about having Captain Briggs and Amy wounded? With all the lead they were spraying around, they'll expect those casualties."

"Next questions: Who do we need to help pull this off, and who can we trust with the info?" asked Sandman.

"The second part's easy," answered Robin. "We trust no one completely. As for the first part, I'm not sure. Ann, any ideas?"

"The President. He should be told, and then he can help control the media. Also, we're going to need him to rope in Highland."

Everyone agreed and decided it was time to quit for the night. If the expected attacks came, it would be a long day. The SEALs knew there was one thing that had to be done before everybody split up. Web looked at Bob with the unspoken question in his eyes.

Bob understood and gave a nod. Web went to his bag and pulled out a bottle of vodka. Without a word he unscrewed the top, took a swig and passed it to Ann. She hesitated for a second, then took a drink and passed it over to Bob.

Silently the bottle was passed around until it got back to Web, who took one last pull and put it back in his bag. The drink sealed the bond; each one of them was now a little less alone in the world. The SEALs had been this way for years, and now their number was doubled. It was no small thing.

The White House, Washington, D.C., 8:00 AM

"Good morning, Mr. President," said Steve Highland, the Secretary of Homeland Security, as he entered the Oval Office. "Thank you for seeing me on such short notice."

"I'm always glad to see you, Steve," replied Woodbird. "Help yourself to some coffee and take a seat. Your call was most fortuitous; I was about to call you."

"What did you want to see me about, Mr. President?"

"It'll wait. What's on your mind?"

"I'm concerned that Admiral Gallaher is not effectively handling this crisis. The four attacks have closed eight major ports, and the country is losing almost two billion dollars a day because of it. The stock markets are in free fall, security at the airports is so tight it's scaring passengers away, and our enemies are laughing at us while rallying support for a Holy War."

"I know all this, Steve, but go on," said the President, waiting to see where Highland was headed.

Warming to his subject, the Secretary continued, "Sir, Gallaher's had unlimited resources and four days to track down these people. So far, she isn't any further along than she was Sunday afternoon. You know there are more attacks expected this morning. If they're successful, it'll shut this country down. It'll be years before we recover."

"What do you propose?"

"That Admiral Gallaher be removed and I take over running the operation. From what I can gather, she's ignoring the regular channels of information and assistance, and is instead relying on Fletcher, Candler, Briggs, Forrest and some old SEALs."

"Have you talked this over with Admiral Gallaher and Admiral Story?"

"I invited her and the others to meet me last evening to discuss this informally, but they never showed up."

"That's what I wanted to speak to you about. You didn't see the news this morning?" asked the President.

"No, I was trying to reach Gallaher, but I couldn't get through, and no one would tell me where she is."

"The people you just mentioned were ambushed last night. Admiral Gallaher and three SEALs were killed, including Bob Davies, the one who identified the terrorist. Forrest and Briggs were wounded. We didn't release all of the details, just that there had been an accident involving Admiral Gallaher and some friends. We told the press that they'd been on their way to dinner and were injured when their car went off a back road into a ditch."

Trying to repress a smile, Highland said, his voice low, "I had no idea, that's a terrible loss."

"So, you get your wish. As of now, you're in charge of the operation. I suggest that you get to your office quickly so you're there when the terrorist calls."

"Yes, Mr. President, and thank you for this opportunity."

After Highland left, Woodbird pushed a button on his phone. "He's gone."

A side door opened and Ann walked in, accompanied by Bob, Web, and Rico. They had watched the meeting on closed-circuit television.

Bob spoke first. "He knew, or, at the very least, he wasn't surprised."

The President rubbed a hand across his face. "I hate to admit it, but I think you're right. There was a flicker of satisfaction on his face when I told him about the ambush and that you were dead. He took the news too calmly not to have known beforehand."

Ann interjected, "Mr. President, I'm truly sorry about this, but there had to be a leak. We spent several hours last night going over what happened and who would have known about Highland's invitation. It turned out that Highland spent considerable time yesterday afternoon asking questions of low-level personnel. If you ask enough people about something, eventually you get a reasonably accurate picture of what's going on. Up to now, he hadn't shown any real interest in the details of our counter-terrorist activities."

"What about Evelyn LaBlanc?" the President asked. "Highland suggested she be part of the ICS team."

Bob said, "We considered her, but no one knows her, so no one would have answered her questions without checking with their superior officer."

"What had you told her?"

"Only that we suspect there's another motive behind the attacks, and that it involves economic control of certain ports. I had Robin slip that into the ICS meeting yesterday morning," replied Ann. "But LaBlanc is an enigma."

The President went to get more coffee and offered to fill the other's cups. Once that was done, he continued, "You expect attacks this morning. Do you have ideas as to which ports will be hit and how?"

"We narrowed it down to two primary targets: San Diego and the Mississippi just below New Orleans. Navy EOD teams swept the areas and located mines in both. These have been neutralized. In addition, we've prepared for hits on three secondary ones: Philadelphia, Miami, and Charleston," said Ann. "As you've seen, the terrorists strike one port on each coast simultaneously.

"Another important factor is that different methods were used each time they've struck. There are only so many ways you can close a harbor without repeating yourself or using weapons of mass destruction. We've made some drastic changes to our own methods that will surprise people."

Woodbird reflected on the information for a few minutes before replying. "Okay, I'll accept your conclusions. But why wasn't this information included in my briefing papers?"

Web replied, "We didn't know who we could trust, so we made sure nobody got enough good information in time to do anything about it."

Woodbird snapped, "I'm the Commander-in-Chief. Are you saying you didn't trust me?"

Unabashed, Web retorted, "Someone tried to kill us. We don't trust anyone—you included, sir."

Bob stepped in. "Mr. President, the only people who know what really happened last night are the ten of us, Robin's FBI friends who helped clean up the site and got us medical attention, and you."

"How do you know you can trust the FBI people?" the President asked.

"Robin trusts them and we trust Robin, that's all we need to know," answered Bob. "Right now you're the only one outside of our circle who knows the whole story."

No one had ever spoken to the President so bluntly. "I'm not sure I want an answer to this, but I'll ask it anyway. If the information you've given me leaks out, what will you do?"

"We'll plug the leak," replied Gator.

"Is that a threat?"

Rico, who hadn't said anything up to this point, answered softly, "No, Mr. President, that's a promise."

Woodbird looked closely at each of the team for a long minute. "If you don't fear the Office of the President, then heaven help anyone else who crosses your path."

31

Coast Guard Headquarters, 10:00 AM Eastern Time

Mark waited, his face blank, his body relaxed. Highland shifted in his seat, looked around, and drummed his fingers on the table. They were alone in the conference room, but phones with open lines to the Communications Center, the President, and Coast Guard Atlantic and Pacific Area commanders were set up. Invisible to both men were cameras and microphones recording everything that went on, and there was electronic equipment designed to pick up and jam transmissions from non-authorized transmitters. Fletcher and his friends were taking no chances that Highland was wired.

Highland jumped when the phone rang and stabbed the Talk button with his finger. The now familiar voice said, "Fletcher, what's your decision?"

Mark leaned forward in his chair. "The same as two days ago: We won't pay the demands."

"You are a slow learner. The lesson will be repeated until your country has been isolated and bled dry."

"We're not defenseless, so give it your best shot."

"You are more stupid than even I could have imagined. Did last night not teach you that there is no safety or defense?"

"It taught me you are a coward who attacks only the seemingly defenseless."

The voice on the other end raged, "I, a coward? No, Fletcher, it is you who is the coward, fighting only from a distance or cringing behind women when danger approaches. I saw you last night as I have seen you before, hiding when death approaches, watching your friends die without lifting a hand to help them."

"No one died last night," Mark goaded. "You and your assassins fled when we fought back."

"You lie," shouted the voice. "That cow of an admiral was killed, as well as a man I believed already dead, and two of the dogs who served him."

Mark asked, "How do you know of this? Your men ran before our fire."

"It was confirmed by a man who never lies to me."

Satisfied that he'd gotten all the information he could from the terrorist, Mark simply said: "We still won't pay you."

"You have been warned, and now a price for your failure will be taken in blood. We will talk again before the sun sets today."

As the connection was broken, Mark spoke into another phone. "You get all that?"

"Yeah, we got it. The alert's been sent. Everybody knows it won't be long."

The White House Family Quarters, 1:00 PM Eastern Time

"You stopped them," said President Woodbird, addressing the group seated around him. "That was good work."

"Thank you, Mr. President," said Ann for the group. "Lee Hunt's evaluation of the threat proved 100 percent accurate. EOD SWATH crews located the mines and neutralized them with only a minimum disruption to shipping traffic. As Mark predicted, the terrorists didn't attempt secondary attacks this time."

"Also, Amy Forrest and Robin's team uncovered info on LaBlanc that ties her into the attacks."

Woodbird exploded: "Why wasn't I told about LaBlanc at our meeting earlier today? You said then that you didn't have anything."

Untroubled by the President's outburst, Robin repeated what she told Ann the day before, concluding with one new piece of information.

"We did a little sneak-and-peak through Highland's personal files, which he keeps locked up. It confirmed my theory that he's involved in the sex-slave trade. These poor people have been used to suborn a good number of government officials, including congressmen and senators."

"You mean that bastard's blackmailing members of my administration? Why didn't you tell me this earlier, along with the rest of it?"

Gator smiled. "Until we checked the tapes, we couldn't be sure about you."

"You're to turn those tapes over to the FBI immediately. That's an order."

"Nope," replied Gator.

Sandman pitched in: "Tapes? What tapes?"

"Admiral Gallaher, I'm ordering you to have these men transfer custody of the tapes to the FBI."

Ann shook her head, adding: "I'm sorry, Mr. President, I don't think I can do that."

"Anyone outside of our group who knows about the tapes is a danger to us. Remember what we said this morning about plugging leaks? We'd hate to have to start now," Mark said, ending the discussion.

Shaken more than he had been by Rico's earlier promise to plug any leaks, Woodbird went to the sideboard, poured himself a glass of bourbon, and took a long drink.

Regaining his composure, he turned and addressed the group calmly. "I ought to have you all shot, but you're right: We don't know how or by whom the information would be used. Help yourselves to the booze, and then tell me what you plan to do next." He permitted himself a tentative smile. "That is if you think you can trust me."

The Jefferson Hotel, Washington, D.C., 3:00 PM Eastern Time

Agitated almost beyond endurance, Steve Highland stormed into LaBlanc's suite.

"They know everything," he shouted. "What are we going to do?"

"Pour yourself a drink and tell me what's going on." LaBlanc looked toward Goldin. "Please pour me a glass of wine and then join us."

His hand shaking, Highland poured a large drink, spilling the liquor on his shirt as he gulped it down. Refilling the glass, he carried it over to where LaBlanc and Goldin were sitting.

In a husky voice, Highland explained.

LaBlanc sat quietly for a moment, before saying, "There isn't anything linking me to the attacks."

"You don't think so?" asked Highland, regaining some of his composure. "Briggs, Fletcher, and the two unwounded SEALs came to my office an hour ago. They found out that you own Seiako and that you've been personally funding the takeover of Terra Marine and the Mexican project. In addition, thanks to your pet terrorist losing his temper and revealing that he knew Gallaher was dead, Fletcher now suspects me of being a mole."

Highland didn't tell her about Briggs bringing the CD that Demivov tried to blackmail him with in Kosovo. Or that Fletcher had proof they'd found the files and tapes Highland had accumulated as a result of his "escort" service.

Evelyn shrugged. "To repeat myself, there's nothing linking me to the attacks. Each step has been carefully planned with several layers of people between the actions and me. All they have is conjecture, and that won't stand up in a court of law. I've insured there are no witnesses who can jeopardize the operation or me; and I will continue to take all necessary steps to protect my safety. Do you understand what I'm saying?"

Highland took another deep drink.

Seeing the comprehension of her words in his eyes, LaBlanc added, "But you needn't worry about your future. I'll arrange it so you come out the hero we planned you'd be."

Relief flooded through Highland. "The President still isn't going to pay al-Hishma. What will you do when that happens?"

"That, too, will be taken care of. Now, you should be back at Coast Guard headquarters when the next call comes in. We'll meet next week, as usual. Appearances need to be maintained," said LaBlanc with a warm smile.

"Please forgive my earlier outburst. I never really doubted you. I look forward to dinner; we'll have much to celebrate."

Following Highland's departure, Evelyn poured another glass of wine and sat down across from Goldin. "Call Demivov and have him pick up the package. Once you get confirmation that he has it, phone al-Hishma and tell him to call our friends with the news. Also, I'd like a few minutes alone."

"Yes, ma'am, right away."

32

Coast Guard Headquarters, Washington, D.C., 4:30 PM Eastern Time

Mark, Doug, Robin, and Amy were discussing options for the next attacks when the call came in. As with each of the previous calls, it began abruptly.

"Fletcher, the sands are running out. Will you pay for the lessons, or are you willing to face Armageddon?"

Coolly, Mark replied, "You failed this morning as you failed that night in Iraq. Perhaps it is you who is the slow learner, not I. There is nothing you know that is unknown to me, and you have nothing that is of value to me."

"So you have finally learned who I am. Well, perhaps what I have is not of value to you," replied al-Hishma, keeping his temper in check, "but your President might feel differently."

Puzzled, Mark looked at Amy and Doug to see if either knew what al-Hishma was referring to. Both shrugged their shoulders. Mark said, "The President values many things, but none are possessed by you."

"Ah, once again, you prove your ignorance. I possess the Secretary of Homeland Security."

"Wait," snapped Mark, hitting the Hold button on the phone. "What are we going to do about this?" he asked Doug.

"Tell him we need to talk with the President and that he should call back in an hour."

Mark did as instructed.

After a brief pause, al-Hishma replied, "You have thirty minutes to decide. Make the most of them," and disconnected.

Doug said, "This could work out very well for us."

"How so?" Amy asked.

"I'll tell you once we get the President, Ann and the rest of the group on the line."

It took Mark ten of the allotted thirty minutes to get a secure hookup with everybody.

Mark briefed them on the call; when he was done, Doug took over.

"Mr. President, I think this will work to our advantage."

"I don't see how their holding Highland helps us."

"We haven't been able to locate al-Hishma and the others. If we can capture one of them, we'll have a direct link to LaBlanc."

"I still don't see how this helps us," countered Ann.

Doug explained. "By holding Highland hostage, they've given us a reason to pay the ransom. We'll set a trap around that point. Since Mark's been the contact from the start, he's the logical person to deliver the ransom."

Amy objected. "You're using Mark as bait?

His eyes warm with affection and amusement at her response, Mark said, "It's okay, I can't see another way of ending this."

Woodbird confirmed it. "I agree; we'll do it your way. Admiral Gallaher, you're authorized to use any resources you need. Also, I'm authorizing you to use whatever force is necessary to stop the terrorists and their supporters, whoever they may be. I'll send a memo for your eyes only so you have it in writing. Keep me informed of your plans. Good luck to you all."

"Thank you, Mr. President," replied Ann as Woodbird hung up.

Coast Guard Headquarters, Washington, D.C., 5:00 PM Eastern Time

"The word Armageddon is the key, and what al-Hishma can use as a means to achieve it is the first question," Bob said to the team. They were all in a conference room for a brainstorming session about how the terrorists would next attack, along with Admirals Story and James. Admirals Veath and Stuart were video-conferenced in.

"A massive explosion would do the trick," Veath suggested.

"Good thought," replied Doug. "What ships in which ports would do the job?"

On her laptop, Amy pulled up the database showing all inbound and outbound traffic for the next twenty-four hours.

As the information scrolled down the screen, Ann said, "I think we may have overplayed our hand by letting Highland know some of what we know about LaBlanc."

"We had to see if he would cave-in and tell us what he knew or pass it along to LaBlanc," replied Doug. "It was the only way to apply pressure and see if she would back down. No one could have anticipated they'd kidnap him."

"It was a gamble from the start," said Mark. "Like LaBlanc, he's guilty, but we'll never be able to prove it. By kidnapping him, they think we'll believe he wasn't in on it. The arrogance of these people is amazing."

"I've got something," Amy interrupted, "actually, I've got two somethings. Take a look." Using a laser pointer, she highlighted what she'd found on the large screen so everyone could see. Two liquefied natural gas (LNG) tankers where due to arrive the next morning: the *Pleiades* in New York and the *Malaysian Star* in San Francisco.

She explained: "According to a study prepared for the Pentagon, the energy content of a single standard LNG tanker, which carries 125,000 cubic meters of gas, is equivalent to about fifty-five Hiroshima atomic bombs."

"I think you've got it," said Veath. "The question is, how will they get close enough to do any damage? They'll be surrounded by patrol boats and aircraft. The terrorists must know we'll shoot first and ask questions later if any boat comes within two thousand yards. We can also eliminate the use of mines since the approaches are too deep for them to be effective, and we can have MCM vessels well ahead of the LNGs."

"Air assault?" suggested Ken James. "Bring in the team by helicopter and have them rappel into the ship's bridge. I'd keep the helo overhead to spot any counter-assault attempts. If they're really smart, there'd be an armed man in the back, ready to take out the LNG if, for some reason, the team was neutralized."

"That would work," answered Stewart, "if they could somehow get past our patrols."

"If I were them, I'd come in low and fast, and then pop up almost alongside," Bob said. "Even if you spotted them coming in, your helos aren't equipped for air-to-air missiles, and you couldn't use them anyway, for fear of hitting the ship. The same goes for the patrol boats."

"And we couldn't use our Maritime Security Response Teams to counter-assault because they'd be shot down, or the terrorists could blow the ship up before we could get close," concluded Ken James.

"Then how do we stop the terrorists?" asked Robin.

Mark said, "We'll use their tactics."

All eyes turned to Fletcher.

"What do you have in mind?" Ann asked.

Mark outlined his ideas.

FRIDAY

Atlantic Ocean, 60 miles southeast of New York, 2:00 AM

Fortunately the seas were calm when the ships met. Boats shuttled back and forth, transferring personnel, while overhead a helicopter placed two louvered boxes on top of the larger ship's superstructure. All messages between the ships were sent in Morse code, using hooded lights, the only completely secure means of communications in this electronic age.

When everything was complete and the ships diverged, the smaller one sent: "Good hunting."

U.S. Coast Guard Station, Sandy Hook, New Jersey, 4:00AM

"Waiting is always the hardest part," Mark said to Amy, who watched in silence as Mark carefully worked over the ammunition in front of him. Off to one side, Gunners Mate Second Class Larry Katula meticulously checked his own weapon.

Satisfied with what he had done, Mark loaded bullets into the magazine and slipped it into his pistol.

"Is there any other way to do this?" Amy asked. "I think you're making too many assumptions about what's going to happen."

"I know, but from what we've learned, this is the most likely scenario."

Amy didn't have an answer and the silence returned.

Verrazano Narrows, New York Harbor, 8:30 AM

Skimming just above the wave tops, Vreeland waited until the last minute before popping up over the stern of the liquefied natural gas tanker. The helicopter's sudden appearance caught the escorting Coast Guard helicopter and patrol boats by surprise. Even if they had seen him, there wasn't anything they could have done. No one was crazy enough to start shooting near a loaded LNG.

Using rappelling ropes, eight people dropped from the helicopter onto the ship and split up. Ryse, Vreeland and four others went to the Bridge. The remaining two secured ropes to the Flying Bridge rail and rappelled down to the catwalk leading across the tops of the five hemispheric-shaped LNG tanks. Reaching the nearest tank, the first attacker unlimbered a shoulder-held antitank weapon and aimed it at the next tank in line. His companion continued to the forward-most tank, several hundred feet away, and pointed his anti-tank weapon at the tank behind him.

The assault team was holding three crewmembers at gunpoint when Ryse and Vreeland entered the Bridge. The Bridge crew consisted of the helmsmen, the ship's captain and the harbor pilot, who leaned heavy on his cane.

"Do as you are told, and you will not be killed," Ryse lied. At this point he could not afford to have trouble; none of his people knew how to handle a ship. Later, it wouldn't make any difference. Pointing to two of his team, he ordered, "Search these three and let them get back to their jobs." Vreeland and the third attacker headed down to secure the rest of the crew.

While one of the two terrorists covered the men from the side, the second one, a woman, conducted the search. After patting down his arms and legs, she reached to check the helmsman's crotch. As she did so, he leered at her and said, "Hey, pretty lady, you looking for a handful? How about a mouthful? We can get it on here or someplace a little more private. I'll stuff your pussy with all you could ever want."

Enraged, one of the assault team drove his rifle into the helmsman's kidneys. The helmsman grunted and fell to his knees. "Watch your mouth or I'll kill you."

The woman finished her search, not touching the man's crotch. The captain carried a pocketknife; the only other metal on him was an ornate belt buckle. After a thorough search that yielded nothing dangerous, the pilot was allowed to retrieve his cane.

From a radio mounted at the back of the Bridge came repeated calls from the senior Coast Guard escort demanding to know what was going on. Picking up the handset, Ryse said, "I have taken control of the vessel, and have positioned people with anti-tank weapons to blow it up. Also, we hold Secretary Highland hostage and will kill him at the slightest sign of resistance. Do you understand?"

"I understand," came the reply. "What do you want?"

"First, withdraw all of the patrol boats and the helicopter," demanded Ryse. "Next, have Lieutenant Fletcher call me on this frequency. If you do not reach him within five minutes, I will execute a crew member. Is that clear?"

"That's clear," answered the escort commander, and said to one of the crew, "Have the other boats move out and request the helo return to base." Selecting an encrypted radio, he called, "Coast Guard Station Sandy Hook, this is Escort One. Terrorists have taken over the LNG. They are demanding to talk with a Lieutenant Fletcher on Channel 16. Over."

"Escort One, this is Fletcher. I'm coming up on Channel 16 now. Out." Changing radios, Mark said, "This is Fletcher, what do you want?"

"Your presence on this ship within thirty minutes. Bring with you the information you need to transfer the one billion dollars to me. Have an unarmed helicopter bring you. I do not have to tell you the consequences should you fail to arrive."

"It will take me more than thirty minutes to get there."

"That is a lie, and you must be taught not to lie. I know you are in New York, so thirty minutes is enough time."

"Alright, I'll be there."

Ryse turned to Vreeland and said, "He has no guts. What he did to me in Iraq was the act of a coward. Tell the helo crew what's going on and them have him remain close by."

San Francisco Bay, 5:45 AM (8:45 AM Eastern Time)

All Lokesh could see was the LNG tanker's superstructure looming up out of the fog bank ahead of him. The fog kept his helicopter hidden from the patrol boats under them. When he was six miles west of the Golden Gate Bridge, Lokesh keyed the intercom. "We have half an hour to get things set here. With the fog, they'll never know what hit them."

"Excellent," replied Akbar, "we are ready to deploy. I will leave Amund here to deal with any threats. I do not want to have to go for another swim."

Smiling at the response, Lokesh brought the helo into a hover over the superstructure. As the helo's forward motion stopped, the five-man assault team kicked the rappelling lines out and slid to the deck thirty feet below.

"On deck," reported Akbar into his headset. "We will see you in thirty minutes."

"Roger," replied Lokesh, diving back into the protective fog.

On the tanker, two men headed for the Bridge while the others went to place explosive charges around the LNG tanks.

None of the five saw the shapes shadowing them.

34

Verrazano Narrows, New York Harbor, 9:00 AM

The ship was almost under the Verrazano Narrows Bridge when the Coast Guard helicopter appeared. Using the winch mounted in the side door, Mark was lowered to the deck, where he was met and searched before being escorted to the Bridge.

Once there, the guard handed Mark's pistol to Ryse. Ryse looked at it for a moment, checked to make sure there was a round in the chamber, and pointed it at Mark. "It has been a long time, Lieutenant, but I am pleased to see you brought this with you. It will make our meeting more interesting."

Highland stood beside Ryse, his face pale, not sure of his role in this scenario.

Not getting a reply, Ryse continued, "Let's get the transfer done. But, before we do, you will learn the price of lying to me." He placed Mark's pistol against Highland's forehead and pulled the trigger.

Mark didn't react to the execution. In his mind, it was the traitor's just reward.

Ignoring the body, Vreeland stepped forward with a laptop computer while Mark pulled a similar one from his bag. When both were logged into their respective banks, the transfer began, and the men watched as both screens tracked the transaction.

They were standing to one side of the Bridge, away from the others. Mark looked around, noting that each of the three civilians had a terrorist guard standing behind him.

San Francisco Bay, 6:00 AM (9:00 AM Eastern Time)

Racing down the ladder, Akbar reached the Bridge and smashed the door open. Instead of docile civilians, Akbar was astounded to see armed men blocking his way.

"It's a trap!" he shouted into his head set, firing at the figure in front of him. "Kill them, kill them all!" he commanded moments before a bullet mushroomed in his chest, killing him. The second man dropped his weapon and surrendered. On the main deck, the other three attackers were ambushed and subdued without a shot being fired.

Hovering in the fog, Lokesh was stunned by Akbar's report and the sound of gunfire coming in over the radio. He headed back to help his friend.

"Amund, get ready to fire an RPG as soon as we're over the target," he said. "Shoot into a tank. If we can't blow them up, maybe we can burn them up."

Two U.S. Coast Guard armed helicopters were waiting when he pulled clear of the fog. He saw them just as his earphones came to life.

"Rogue copter, this is Coast Guard Helo Three-Five. You will proceed to Oakland Airport and land where instructed. You will comply immediately with this order. Do you understand?"

Lokesh knew Americans never shot down unarmed aircraft. Keying the intercom once more, he said: "Take out the nearest helo."

Amund was swinging his weapon around when a tongue of fire lashed out from a third, unseen Coast Guard helo. The stream of lead cut Lokesh's helo apart, the pieces falling unheeded into the fog-shrouded ocean.

Verrazano Narrows, New York Harbor, 9:15 AM

"Man, what's taking so long?" said Walters, the assault helo pilot over the intercom to his gunner. "My butt hurts and the fuel's getting low." He'd been circling the tanker for forty-five minutes, alternately scanning the sky and his instruments.

"We've got company at four o'clock," reported the gunner.

Walters looked over his right shoulder and saw a small, brightly painted helicopter headed towards him. Banking the helo to get a better look, Walters noticed it belonged to a local news station and a large camera was pointed at the tanker.

Keying his mike, Walters said, "What the hell are you doing here? Leave now or I'll knock you out of the sky."

"Hey, lover," said a female voice, "give me a break, I'm only trying to do my job. Do you have any idea what I went through to get here?"

Walters watched as the other helo dropped slightly below him, apparently trying to get a close-up of the ship. "I don't know and I don't care. Now get out."

"Okay, okay, you don't have to get mad about it, I'm on my way," replied Amy. Switching to the intercom, she said, "On the count of three, I'm going to pull up. Start firing as soon as I do and we'll rip-saw this guy to pieces."

Tightening his grip on the disguised Stinger launcher, Katula replied: "My pleasure, ma'am, my pleasure."

"One. Two. Three!"

Walters's last thought as shells tore through the cockpit was that he'd been fooled by one of his own tricks.

The sound of the helo exploding carried to the ship below. Rico and Sandman, lying on foam pads in the louvered boxes airlifted on board earlier, heard it. Their MK11 Sniper rifles covered the whole forward part of the ship, and, with slight adjustments, they fired. The soft-nosed bullets killed the terrorists instantly.

Concealed in a cabinet at the back of the Bridge, Bob also heard the explosion. Smashing the door aside, he stepped out and snapped a quick shot at Vreeland.

Startled by the explosion and Bob's shot from behind them, the guards were slow to react. The three civilians weren't.

Gator reached into his pants, pulling out the slim automatic pistol hidden there. Turning, he jammed the muzzle into his guard's throat and fired.

"That's two down," he muttered, looking around. He saw Doug release the knife concealed in his belt buckle and, in one fluid motion, slide the blade in behind the second guard's ear.

Gator said, "Nice work, that's a sure place for a quick kill."

As he pointed the cane at the last guard and pulled the concealed trigger, Web said, "Good help is so hard to find these days." The small caliber slug hit the woman in the head, ending all she was or ever would be.

Vreeland was bringing his submachine gun up when Bob's bullet struck him. Reflexively, Vreeland pulled the trigger of his weapon, sending bullets through the confined space.

Ryse looked up from the computer as Katula fired.

"Betrayed!" he screamed, shooting Mark repeatedly with the heavy pistol. But no blood erupted as the bullets tore into Mark.

Pulling the knife from its sheath behind his neck, Mark said, "I took most of the powder out of the shells, knowing you would shoot me with my own weapon. There was enough to kill close up, but that's all." Just as he was advancing on Ryse, searing pains lanced through his left arm when a piece of shrapnel tore open the muscles.

"Now we will fight on even terms," Ryse smiled, pulling his own knife.

Mark backed away, trying to stem the flow of blood. Ryse, moving with easy grace, lunged forward, the tip of his knife slitting Mark's right sleeve. Mark gritted his teeth, fighting against the pain. Risking a glance over his shoulder, Mark saw the others were too far away to help.

Mark warily circled Ryse, who thrust out again, this time nicking Mark's wrist.

Jumping back to avoid the next sweep, Mark slipped on a puddle of his own blood and Ryse embedded his knife in Mark's thigh as he fell. Agony shot through Mark as he rolled over, pinning Ryse's knife in his leg. Through a red haze, he fought to bring his own knife around until the tip rested under his antagonist's chin.

Feeling the point prick his skin, Ryse stopped struggling. Looking into Mark's eyes Ryse jeered, "You will not kill me. You do not have the guts to use a knife."

He felt Mark pull the knife away from his throat. "See," he continued, smiling, "I knew you were a coward."

Mark drove the knife upward. "Wrong again."

35

Seiako Headquarters, New York City, 1:00 PM

Gwen Goldin looked up as Ann and Robin entered the office.

"Is she in?" Ann demanded.

Shocked at seeing Ann alive, Goldin said, "Yes, but Ms. LaBlanc is very busy and you can't go in now. Perhaps if you come back later, she'll have a moment to spare."

Ignoring her, Ann continued towards LaBlanc's office.

Goldin pulled a pistol out of her desk drawer and aimed it at Ann's back. "I told you, you can't go in there now."

Robin pulled her own pistol and shot Goldin.

Ann turned around at the sound of the shot. "Thanks," was all she said, retrieving Goldin's pistol and opening the doors to LaBlanc's office. Robin followed her in.

LaBlanc was stuffing papers into a briefcase.

"What was that noise?" LaBlanc asked, focused on her packing. When she received no response, she looked up. It took her just a second to recover and snap, "I left instructions not to be disturbed. You have no business here, so please leave."

"Al-Hishma is dead, Highland's dead, the two terrorist assault helicopters have been shot down, and the terrorist team members on board the LNGs are dead. Is your thirst for revenge quenched? " Ann growled.

Almost smiling, LaBlanc continued filling her briefcase. "Do you have any proof that I was responsible for the actions of those men?" She looked up, offering an ice-cold glare. "No, you do not. At best there is only conjecture, and that won't stand up in court. Now, if you'll excuse me, I have a flight to catch."

Robin said: "She's right. We've uncovered no evidence linking her to the attacks. Morally she's guilty of hundreds of deaths and the wanton destruction of millions of dollars worth of property, but legally there's no proof."

LaBlanc closed her briefcase and got up to leave. "It's been very interesting working with you both. Now I must go."

Ann said: "Before you go, there is a lesson I wish to teach you."

"Oh?" replied LaBlanc. "I don't believe there is anything you can teach me."

"The lesson I have for you is that you can't get away with murder."

Pointing Goldin's pistol at LaBlanc's head, she pulled the trigger.

AFTERWARD

36

Coast Guard Headquarters, Washington, D.C.

They sat in companionable silence, feeling the week's tensions drain away.

"It's been a hard three months, but I think the storm has subsided," Admiral Vince Story said to Ann.

Breaking her reverie, Ann answered, "Looks that way. We knew it was going to happen, but that didn't make it any easier to go through."

The deaths of Goldin and La Blanc had been reported as a murder/suicide. Few details of the crime were released, and Goldin's motive for killing her employer was left to conjecture.

Highland was given a hero's funeral with a service held in the National Cathedral. President Woodbine delivered the eulogy, praising the secretary for sacrificing himself to save the life of a member of the assault team.

Bob summed up the situation by quoting a former Yugoslav police officer:

"Truth, lies, all same."

There was one aspect of the final recap of the attacks that troubled Ann, and she hadn't been able to resolve it.

An FBI team, accompanied by Doug, had searched Highland's office after the last failed attack. They seized his personal computer, took records from the safe, and located a flash drive taped under a desk drawer.

Through it all, Highland's secretary, Lena, watched, seemingly numbed by the turn of events. When questioned, she said Highland had always been very secretive. He never spoke about his personal life, and he handled his own calendar and email.

No, he hadn't appeared nervous when the attacks were going on—except on Thursday afternoon, just before he went to see Ms. LeBlanc.

Yes, he had asked to use her home for a meeting with Admiral Gallaher, but that was all she knew about it. When asked about the rest of his staff, she replied they were very nice, but she only knew them professionally and didn't socialize with them outside the workplace.

Within twenty-four hours of the FBI's talk with her, Lena Constance disappeared. A search of her house showed she'd left in a hurry, taking only a few things. All attempts to locate her were futile; no one by that name ever existed. Later, reviewing Highland's personal trophy tapes, they found out why: Lena was featured on several of them. It left Ann and the rest with a cold, sick feeling that she had been eliminated for the sake of security.

Another issue that had to be dealt with was Congress. Both the Senate and the House committees held numerous hearings and launched an uncounted number of investigations in an attempt to find someone to blame for the terrorists' attacks, generating the usual sound and fury, but producing nothing of significance.

Anyone probing too deeply was checked against Highland's files, which Davies refused to turn over to the President. If there was a match, he or she received a visit from Bob Davies, during which he suggested that perhaps it would be advisable to back off. Those who weren't receptive were shown clips of their personal file, which generally took care of the problem. The few who proved obstreperous soon found the files leaked to the media, which resolved the issue quickly. It was blackmail, pure and simple, but it worked. Eventually the politicians shifted their attention to other vote-getting topics and the press dutifully followed along.

In addition to Congressional hearings, the Coast Guard and other agencies conducted their own evaluations of the events. The Coast Guard suffered more combat casualties than in all other actions since the end of World War II combined. Reasons for this had to be established before corrective action could be taken.

It was a painful process for all involved. None of the commanders were incompetent nor was the personnel poorly trained. The mistakes had been in the equipment employed by small boat units and the rules under which the people were forced to fight. After attending too many memorial services which proved those points, no one debated the need for change. Through it all, only John Quigley's death required the Commandant's intercession to smother some resentment.

"You and Jessie Veath did the right thing for John Quigley," said Ann. "He deserved to be honored for protecting his crew. Sara Wang told Jessie the whole story, and she feels responsible for John's death. It helped Wang a lot to be the one to spread John's ashes at sea."

"It's sad that Quigley had no family to mourn his passing."

"But, Vince, we all mourned him. For good or bad, he was part of us."

After a taking a moment to relish the truth of that statement, Story moved on. "You and Robin did a good job with Seiako. Of course, they didn't have many options. Still, it's nice to see the right thing being done for the victims."

This was another piece of information known only to the President, Robin Candler, and Admirals Story and Gallaher.

Seiako's Board of Directors had agreed to generously compensate the victims of the attacks and their families. In addition, the company was underwriting the costs of restoring the ports and repairing the facilities damaged by LaBlanc's actions. The monies for this were paid out of several accounts, none of which could be traced to Seiako.

The board was happy to make the deal. Doing the right thing was the alternative to having the company dismembered by their competitors and the international community if word of Seiako's involvement in the attacks leaked out, something that Ann had guaranteed would happen if they didn't cooperate.

Story had one more question: "What about Mark?"

Ann had no answer for him.

37

Harpswell, Maine

Haunted by nightmares, Mark gave up trying to sleep. Wrapping a blanket around his shoulders, he went to the kitchen, brewed a pot of coffee, and sat staring out the east-facing window. His arm and leg healed better than expected, and he needed to make the decision soon whether to stay in the Coast Guard or get out—but he wasn't doing it that day.

After leaving the hospital almost two months ago, Mark hadn't heard from Doug, Robin, Admiral Gallaher, any of the SEALs or Amy. Amy visited him a few times while he was in the hospital, but the visits were a strain on them both. She'd sent him a get-well card a week after his discharge, but there was no return address, so he couldn't write back. No one in the Coast Guard would tell him where she was or what she was doing. Eventually, he gave up trying to reach her.

He loved her and had been in love with her almost from the moment they met. What had he done to drive her away? The last time he saw her in the hospital, he tried to tell her about his feelings, but she changed the subject and left shortly afterward. Apparently Amy didn't love him, and it hurt worse than getting shot.

Mark felt his spirits rise as the sun crept up from the indigo sea, streaking the horizon with wondrous colors. After a week of rain, the cold and damp finally gave way to a beautiful Indian summer day.

With his lifting spirits came the decision to take the boat out for the first time in months. Dressing quickly, Mark tucked his pistol into a pocket and walked to the marina. Once there, it only took a few minutes to check over the sailboat.

Heading down the bay, feeling the wind caress his face and the easy motion through the swell, Mark realized how much he'd missed the water. Sailing on the bay was always a joy, one he had briefly forgotten about.

It was mid-morning before he returned to the marina, refueled the boat, and headed home. Approaching the house, he saw an SUV parked in the driveway. Drawing the pistol from his jacket pocket, Mark faded into the woods to evaluate the situation. No one ever came there without an invitation, and there'd been no calls. As he surveyed what he could see of the outside of the house, he smelled coffee.

Bad guys setting up an ambush won't leave their van in plain sight or brew coffee, so Mark put the pistol away and went in. Voices came from the enclosed porch overlooking the bay.

When he got to the porch doorway, he saw Bob sitting next to Ann on the couch while Robin and Doug occupied deck chairs.

"It's about time," Bob said. "If you weren't back in another ten minutes, we were going to call the Coast Guard."

Mark stood there, momentarily speechless.

"This is the first time all of us have had a chance to get away." Robin grinned. "Ann flew Doug and me up to Provincetown where we shanghaied Bob."

With a concerned look on her face, Ann said, "Mark, we're sorry to just drop in. We wanted to see how you're doing."

A big smile slowly covered Mark's face. "I'm really glad to see you, and you picked a terrific time to show up. It's been rough, but I'm through it. And now that you're here, anybody got any ideas for what to do this weekend?"

From behind him a quiet voice asked: "How about a beach party?"

Turning around slowly, Mark gently gathered Amy into his arms and finally had the chance to say: "I love you."

With infinite tenderness, she hugged him back. "I love you too."

For a long time they held each other, together at last and finally at peace with all that had happened. Keeping his arm around Amy, Mark turned back to his friends.

"A beach party sounds good," he said in a husky voice. "Hey, Go-Go, how about you buy the beer, I drive the boat?"

ABOUT MIKE WALLING

Before I was 30, I'd been in everything from an Arctic hurricane to a rum factory in Haiti.

I've been blessed by the Northern Lights, sailed through Prince Christian Sound at the tip of Greenland, seen the Green Flash as the sun set behind the Leeward Islands, and watched dolphins play in a tug's bow wave in the Gulf of Mexico.

The terms 'Boarding Party' and 'Prize Crew' evoke images of pirates and bloody cutlasses. Reality for me was a .45 pistol and backed up by M16's and .50 caliber machine guns.

One time on ship if I had zigged instead of zagged, they would have buried me in two pieces."

All this and a buck gets me a cup of coffee.

On a more serious note, Mike served for six years in the U.S. Coast Guard as a commissioned officer and a senior petty officer. His assignments included buoy tending, search and rescue missions, drug law enforcement, and oceanographic operations in the Arctic. As part of the Boarding Party and Prize Crew teams on two cutters, he participated in the seizures of a Panamanian drug-runner and a Cuban fishing boat.

He is an internationally known author, historian, and researcher. In addition to military history, his recognized expertise includes global security, counter terrorism, transnational crime, and human trafficking.

His first book, *Bloodstained Sea: The U.S. Coast Guard in the Battle of the Atlantic 1941-1944*, was published by International Marine, a division of McGraw-Hill, and received critical acclaim by reviewers and veterans. The Naval Order of the United States honored him with its 2005 Samuel Eliot Morison Award for Naval Literature.

Mike published a new edition of *Sinbad of the Coast Guard* (Flat Hammock Press, Mystic, 2005), a book for young readers about the adventurous true story of the USCGC *Campbell*'s mascot whose exploits during World War II became legend. The original appeared in 1945 and has been out of print for almost sixty years.

He and Mary live in Hudson, Massachusetts. Mike may be reached through his website: www.mikewalling.com or www.cutterpublishing.com.

Made in the USA